U0032553

讀李家同學英文 3

李家同◎著

Nick Hawkins（郝凱揚）◎翻譯　　周正一◎解析

I'm Only
Eight Years Old
我只有八歲

序

李家同

　　我真該謝謝郝凱揚先生將我的文章譯成了英文。這當然不是一件簡單的事情,但是我看了他的翻譯,我發現他的翻譯是絕對正確的,而且非常優美。外國人寫的小說,往往用字非常艱難。對一般人而言,都太難了。這本書比較容易,沒有用太難的字。郝先生是美國人,能做這件事情,充分展現他的中英文造詣很高,他一定是一位非常聰明的人。

　　這一本書最大的好處是有對英文的註解、也有練習,想學英文的年輕人可以從註解中學到很多英文的基本學問。

　　我在此給讀者一個建議:你不妨先看看中文文章,先不看英文的翻譯,然後試著將中文翻成英文,我相信你一定會覺得中翻英好困難。翻完以後,再去看郝先生的翻譯,相信你可以學到不少,也可以寫出越來越像外國人寫的句子。

　　我尤其希望讀者注意標點符號的用法。英文的標點符號是非常重要的,中文句子,對標點符號的標準比較寬鬆,但英文絕對不行,一個標點符號用錯了,全句的結構就是錯了。讀者可以利用這個機會好

好地學會如何正確地下英文的標點符號。

另外，千萬要注意動詞的用法，如果你英文動詞沒有錯，你的英文就很厲害了。信不信由你，英文不好的人常常不會用現在完成式，可是這本書裡用了很多的現在完成式，你不妨仔細研究為什麼要用這種我們中國人所不熟悉的時態。

在英文句子裡，一定要有一個主詞和一個動詞，讀者不妨在每一個句子裡去找一下，主詞和動詞一定會存在。我們中國人有時會寫一個英文句子，但是句子中，主詞和動詞弄不清楚，以至於有的動詞沒有主詞。也就因為如此，凡是這種主詞和動詞關係不清楚的句子，意思也會弄不清楚。讀者如果覺得這些文章很容易懂，其實完全是因為每一個句子的主詞和動詞都很清楚的原因。

如果你有時不知道如何用英文表達你的想法，你應該知道，這是正常的事。多看這本書，對你一定有幫助。

看這本書的時候，再次建議你先看中文，立刻試譯，再參考英譯。這樣做，對你的英文作文會有很大的好處。

最後我謝謝周先生，他的註解使這本書生色不少。當然我也該謝謝聯經出版公司，我相信這本書的出版會有助於很多想學好英文的年輕人，這本書能夠順利出現，林載爵先生和何采嬪女士有很大的功勞，我在此謝謝他們。

起而行

郝凱揚

　　李家同令人敬佩的地方，不在於他淵博的學問，也不在於他虔誠的信仰。我之所以佩服他，是因為他將他的理想付諸行動。

　　眾人皆知，李教授信奉的是天主教，而且他以他的信仰為寫作的出發點。在台灣，即使把天主教、基督教和摩門教三大派基督徒的人數全部加起來，所佔的比例還不到人口的一成。那麼，一個天主教徒寫的書怎麼會在台灣的社會廣受歡迎呢？關鍵在於「付諸行動」四個字。

　　幾年前，我在台灣當過兩年的傳教士。當我問人家「你有什麼宗教信仰」時，最常聽到的一句話是「所有的宗教都是勸人為善」。其實我並非不知道，說這句話的用意是以較為委婉的口氣拒絕我，但這十一個字所蘊含的意義非常深刻。儒家的「仁義」、道家的「道」、佛教的「慈悲」、基督徒的「博愛」、甚至無神論的「倫理」，宗旨都不外乎教人把內在的善性發揮出來。然而光說好聽的話沒有用——真正的信徒一定要實踐他的信仰，否則他只是個偽善者。李家同主要不是個作者，乃是個「做者」：文作得少，事做得多。也就是因為如此，才有這麼多的讀者閱讀他的書，並從中得到感動。

　　「實踐」是個極為管用的通則，我們不妨想想它如何適用在語言的學習上。假如一個人（我們不說他是誰）訂了一年的美語雜誌，每個月固定讀一本上好的英文教材，但他從來不寫半個英文字，也不說半句英語，試問，他的英文能力會突飛猛進嗎？他對自己的英文能力會有很大的信心嗎？我再來做另一個假設：倘若另一個人（我們依然不說他是誰）買不起最好的英文教材，但他喜歡跟幾個不會中文的外國朋友見面，也喜歡寫英文日記或部落格，那麼英文會不會豐富他的人生？他會不會比較容易記住他所學的東西？

　　你自己比較像這兩個人中的哪一個？如果你的答案令你不滿，你要如何改變你學英文的方式？以我學中文的經驗來說，我覺得最重要的是給自己一個愛學的理由和非練習不可的環境。愛學的理由可以好玩（想唱美國的流行音樂）；文雅（更能欣賞英國文學）；不良（可以搭訕外國女生）；實際（要跟國際的客戶做生意）；無聊（愛挑布希總統的語病）等等，找自己的理由應該不難。尋找非練習不可的環境對無法長期出國的人可能沒那麼容易，可是並非不可能──除了以上提過的，和不會中文的外國人交朋友以及利用網路寫英文部落格，還有別的方法。還有，在學會講英文的過程中，一定要多出一些難堪的錯，發現了之後笑一笑自己，因為這樣才算豁了出去。如果你因為怕出糗而只講最簡單的英文，怎麼會進步？你又不是沒聽過四聲不準的外國學生說「我恨矮台灣人」（我很愛台灣人）啦！

　　最後我想說，我絕對不是個隨隨便便的譯者──把這些精采的故事譯成傳神的英文花了我不少心思。目的只有一個──希望你能藉此體會到英文的樂趣！至於進步，我和解析者周正一先生只能提供好的資源──要不要好好利用，完全由你決定了。

「小試身手」的題目設計

周正一

　　「讀李家同學英文」系列已經邁入第三輯,每次新的一輯出書,當然心情隨之雀躍萬分,畢竟,其中也包含了自己的努力。

　　解析工作苦甜參半,甜的一面,是李教授自然而感人的故事提升了我的中文寫作能力,以及郝先生的英譯更讓原本研習翻譯的我,對英文的思考模式有更進一步的理解,這些都是在解析過程中的收穫。

　　當然解析工作過程也有艱辛的一面,其中尤以設計「小試身手」的題目為最。

　　我寫解析的過程是,在英譯中找到適合解析的句型或文法要點,將句型加以整理,把文法觀念做過闡釋,接下來就是要設計配合重點、讓讀者透過練習而加深印象的「小試身手」。多半我會先把英文句子寫好,然後再配上中文。這當中有兩個需要考量的問題:

一、難度

　　根據英譯的難度,這個系列的讀者層,英文程度應該在高中及高中以上。所以不能太淺易,以免沒有效果;但是題目若太難,又可

能重創讀者信心。因此,難易之間頗難拿捏。平心而論,有些題目真的稍具難度,不容易下手。即使是我自己設計的題目,在過一段時間後,連我自己也沒有把握寫出一樣好(或者一樣爛)的答案。像是:

> 18-1. 以他獲得諾貝爾獎的年紀而論,我們應該加倍推崇他。〈三個孩子的故事〉
>
> Considering the age at which he won the Nobel prize, we ought to respect him even more.

不過,極具難度的題目仍屬少數。我相信從第一輯到第三輯,有些題目真的是需要讀者翻字典查找所需的字詞,甚至和他人討論。只是這又何妨,查字典和就教他人,其實不就是學英文的正途嗎?而且,一個意念,可能有多種表達方式,書中所附的答案,只是若干表達方式的其中一種,讀者自行「研發」的答案,雖不中亦不遠矣,說不定比參考答案更好。

二、方向

題目內容是天文地理?還是人事歷史?在這方面我的想法是,既然多數人學英文的目標是為了能夠應用,而應用大抵脫離不了生活。因此,在做法上就盡量朝「生活應用」這個目標走。有些題目的靈感常常從生活中得來,比如以下這個題目的設計時間,剛好台北市政府正在舉辦一年一度的牛肉麵節活動,就順勢把它融入解析重點,而設計出如下的題目:

> 16. 上不了網,我沒辦法知道哪家餐廳料理最好的牛肉麵。〈三個孩子的故事〉

Without Internet access, I have no way of knowing which restaurant serves the best beef noodles.

有時候我們也來點勵志性質的東西。眾所週知，學習英語是條漫長而辛苦的路程，需要投注大量的時間和恆心。所以我們會適時給讀者如下的題目。

27. 在他們看來，持之以恆是學習新語言成功最重要的因素。〈週五的夢魘〉

In their eyes, perseverance is the most vital factor in learning a new language successfully.

最後要向讀者們說，有時因為句型本身的關係，以致於題目頗有難度，功力不夠深厚的讀者會深感挫折，如果你有這種感覺，請接受我最深的歉意。但是我建議你，不要因此而放棄，看看優美的文章，欣賞流暢的英譯，或者只閱讀解析的部分。甚至偷懶一下，只思考中文題目，再翻翻解答……，不管怎樣的接觸型態，都會讓你有所得、有所進步。

目次
CONTENTS

The Friday Nightmares
週五的夢魘

1-5　　所有認識張總經理的人都會佩服他的才能。他有一點特點：凡是他想學的他都會學得非常好。

　　舉例來說，在中學的時候他不僅功課非常好，連體育都非常好，如果他肯的話，他可以參加很多校隊，進了台大念電機系以後，他仍然是出人頭地，大多數同學應付考試都來不及，他卻有時間注意各種新技術的發展。難怪他在柏克萊念研究所的時候不僅指導教授喜歡他，矽谷很多公司也都喜歡他。他的指導教授號稱會滑雪，他三下兩下就滑得非常好。

　　在柏克萊拿到博士學位以後，總經理回國了。大多數有博士頭銜的人喜歡去大學教書，他卻進入工業界服務，從普通的工程師做起，一帆風順地做到了我們公司的總經理。

CD1-3
◇ admire（v.）欽佩
◇ talent（n.）才氣；天份；才華
◇ unique [ju`nik]（adj.）獨具的
◇ trait（n.）（人格）特質
◇ exceptionally（adv.）格外地
◇ middle school 中學
◇ outstanding（adj.）傑出的；出色的
◇ athlete（n.）運動員
◇ electrical engineering department 電機系
◇ grad student 研究生（研究所學生）
◇ advisor（n.）（研究論文）指導老師

Everyone who knew General Manager Zhang admired him for his talents. He had a unique trait: no matter what it was that he wanted to learn how to do, he'd learn to do it exceptionally well.

1-5

CD1-1

For example, in middle school, he was not only an outstanding student but an outstanding athlete as well—had he wanted to, he could have played on many school athletic teams. Even after getting into the electrical engineering department of National Taiwan University, he was still a cut above the rest. Most of his classmates were so busy that they had their hands full just trying to pass their exams, but he had the time to pay attention to all sorts of new technological developments. Small wonder that when he was a grad student at UC Berkeley, he wasn't just well-liked by his advisor, but by a lot of companies in Silicon Valley as well. His advisor claimed to be a skier; after just a few runs down the mountain, old Zhang could ski very well too.

After getting his doctorate at Berkeley, the general manager returned to his native country. Most Ph.D. holders like to get jobs teaching at universities, but old Zhang entered the manufacturing sector. He started out as an ordinary engineer but quickly rose to become the general manager of our company.

◇ Silicon Valley 矽谷(在美國加州，為半導體高科技之重鎮)
◇ doctorate (n.)博士學位
◇ native country 本國；母國；原居國
◇ Ph.D. holder 獲有博士學位的人(Ph. D. 即 Doctor of Philosophy，俗稱「博士」)
◇ manufacturing sector 製造業

　　我們大家都佩服他，可是我們都全體一致地討厭他，因為張總經理是完全沒有什麼同情心的人，對於任何能力差的人，他一概毫不保留地表示他的輕視。他自己太能幹，所以他很難理解為何有人會表現得如此不理想。他常常告訴我，他認為優勝劣敗是自然界的最高法則。能力差的人絕對應該讓路，使能力高的人能夠掌握社會。

　　他本來很欣賞老王的，因為他看過老王設計的電路，發現老王能力很強。可是他和老王見面以後，才發現老王是位殘障人士，走路必須用拐杖。張總經理走路非常快，老王根本趕不上他。他又從不肯自己放慢腳步，搞到最後，老王每次和他一齊走的時候，都會遙遙落後，最後只好換了一家公司做事。

6-10　　小李是他的司機，替他開了六年半的車，他從來沒有和他談過一句閒話，即使兩小時的車程，他也不會和他談一句話。

◇ devoid（adj.）空無的；沒有的
◇ sympathy（n.）同情心
◇ reservation（n.）保留
◇ contempt（n.）藐視；輕蔑
◇ inferior（adj.）較差的；較低劣的
◇ tremendous（adj.）巨大的；驚人的
◇ virtually（adv.）幾乎；幾近
◇ inept（adj.）愚驗的；笨拙的
◇ principle（n.）原則；原理
◇ survival（n.）生存
◇ self-evident（adj.）自明的；明明白白的
◇ untalented（adj.）沒有才華的

We all admired him, but not one of us liked him, for General Manager Zhang was utterly devoid of sympathy. He had absolutely no reservations about expressing his contempt for anyone of inferior ability. His tremendous talent made it virtually impossible for him to understand why there were people who were so seemingly inept. He often told me how he thought that the highest principle in nature was the survival of the fittest. To him, it was self-evident that untalented people ought to step aside and let the more capable take the reins of society.

He used to really like Old Wang because he could tell from the circuits he designed that he was quite talented. But when he met him in person, he discovered that Old Wang was handicapped: he had to walk with a cane. General Manager Zhang was a very fast walker, and although Old Wang couldn't keep up with him, he refused to slacken his pace. The result was that every time Old Wang walked with him, he'd fall way behind. In the end, all he could do was find another company to work for.

Little Li had been his chauffeur for six and a half years, but the boss had never once struck up a casual conversation with him, not even on a two-hour car ride.

6-10

◇ capable(adj.)有能力的；能幹的
◇ rein(n.)韁繩(此處用在片語 take the reins of 以表示「駕馭」、「掌控」)
◇ circuit [ˋsɝkɪt](n.)電路
◇ design(v.)設計
◇ talented(adj.)有才華的；有天份的
◇ handicapped(adj.)殘障的
◇ slacken(v.)放慢；鬆懈
◇ chauffeur [ˋʃofɚ](n.)私家車司機
◇ casual(adj.)隨意的

　　老張是我認識的人之中最有自信的人，這也難怪他，他從小就不知道什麼叫做「失敗」，大多數高中生功課好的話，體育就奇差，體育好的傢伙卻大多只是四肢發達、頭腦簡單，只有老張，教室裡的考試他不怕，連操場裡的各種考試也都難不倒他。也就因為如此，對於任何表現不好的人，他會打從心裡有一種厭惡的心理，而且也常將這位倒楣鬼開除掉。

　　兩個月前，老張和我在他辦公室討論一件事，我的一個同事老陳敲門進來，老陳才能中等，可是做事十分認真，因為勤能補拙，他的表現還不錯，可憐的是，他前一陣子母親病重，老陳常要去照顧他的母親，有些事情當然做得不太好。老陳一進來就結結巴巴地向總經理承認自己在電路設計的工作上進度落後，都是因為母親生病的原因。他母親已去世，他應該可以彌補過去的時間，將進度趕上。

　　別人一聽到老陳的母親去世，都會稍微表示一點同情之意。老張卻不如此，他說任何人表現不好，就應該滾蛋，不論什麼理由，因為公司的工作進度落後，損失很大。他又說我們公司只需要會做事的

◇ confident (adj.) 有自信的
◇ blame (v.) 責怪；怪罪
◇ excel [ɪkˋsɛl] (v.) 勝出；超越
◇ lousy (adj.) 差勁的；糟糕的
◇ dumb (adj.) 愚笨的；遲鈍的
◇ despise (v.) 輕視；藐視
◇ substandard (adj.) 未達標準的
◇ coworker (n.) 同事

Old Zhang was the most confident person I knew, and it was hard to blame him—ever since he was born, he had never known the meaning of the word "failure". Back then, most high school students who excelled academically were lousy at gym, while the athletic guys tended to be dumb jocks. Only Old Zhang feared neither exams in the classroom nor whatever physical tests he might face in gym. Therefore, he genuinely despised anyone who did substandard work, and he'd often fire the poor fellow.

Two months ago, Old Zhang and I were discussing something in his office when Old Chen, a coworker of mine, knocked on the door and came in. Old Chen was a man of average ability, but he was a hard worker, and since diligence can compensate for clumsiness, he had always performed pretty well. Unfortunately, not long ago, his mother had fallen very ill. Old Chen often had to go care for her, so naturally there were a few jobs he hadn't been doing so well on. As soon as Old Chen walked in, he stammeringly admitted to the general manager that he had fallen behind in his circuit design work because his mother had been sick, but now that she had passed away, he felt sure he could make up for lost time and get caught up on his work.

Anyone else would have shown a little sympathy upon learning that Old Chen's mother had passed away, but not Old Zhang. He said that anyone who did poor work for any reason should get the hell out, because the company loses a lot of money when it falls behind

◇ average(adj.)平庸的
◇ diligence(n.)勤奮；努力
◇ compensate(for)(v.)補償；彌補
◇ clumsiness(n.)笨拙；遲鈍
◇ perform(v.)做(事)；表現
◇ stammeringly(adv.)結結巴巴地；口齒不清地

人。對於老陳，他已通知人事室，今天是他工作的最後一天，請他去人事室辦離職手續。

老陳是一位非常老實的人，這個被開除的打擊對他當然很大，他有一分鐘的時間說不出一句話來，大概他也知道對張總經理這種人，懇求他開恩是做不到，所以他就一言不發地離開了。

11-15　　他走到門口的時候，忽然回過頭來問，「今天星期幾？」張總經理說：「星期五」，老陳以很嚴肅的口氣說：「好吧，以後我每個星期五晚上都會來找你。」然後他就開門離開了。

我也不懂老陳的話什麼意思，可是我注意到我們的張總經理臉上露出了一絲恐懼的表情。當時我很奇怪，他怕什麼呢？溫和的老陳一定是說說而已，有什麼怕的。

接下去的幾個星期，張總經理變了，他過去是位非常鎮靜的人，自

◇ notify（v.）通知；告知
◇ HR department 人事處（室）（HR 為 Human Resources 的簡寫）
◇ termination paperwork 離職手續（termination 本指「結束」、「終止」，而 paperwork 為「公文」、「文書」之意）
◇ obviously（adv.）顯然地；顯而易見地
◇ speechless（adj.）無言的

in its work. "Our company only wants people who do their jobs," he said. As for Old Chen, he had already notified the HR department that today would be his last day at work. He invited him to head over there to take care of his termination paperwork.

Old Chen was not a man to hide his true feelings; being fired like this was obviously a great blow to him. For a full minute he stood, speechless. Then, probably because he knew it was useless to plead for mercy with someone like General Manager Zhang, he left without a word.

After he had walked to the doorway, he suddenly turned around and asked, "What's today?" "Friday," replied General Manager Zhang. In a deadly serious tone, Old Chen said, "All right then, from now on I'll come looking for you every Friday night." Then he opened the door and left. `11-15`

I didn't understand what Old Chen meant by what he said, but I noticed a trace of alarm on General Manager Zhang's face. I was mystified—what was he afraid of? Mild-mannered Old Chen was just blowing smoke—there was nothing to fear.

But during the few weeks that followed, General Manager Zhang changed. Before, he had always been calm and collected, but after

---

◇ plead (v.) 懇求
◇ mercy (n.) 慈悲；憐憫
◇ deadly (adv.) 非常
◇ tone (n.) 聲調
◇ trace (n.) 痕跡；微量
◇ mystified (adj.) 糊塗的；搞不清楚的
◇ mild-mannered (adj.) 態度溫和的
◇ collected (adj.) 鎮定的；不慌亂的

從那天以後，他變得有些暴躁，而且常常顯得疲倦，開會時也心不在焉。尤其最怪的是，他在每個週五的下午表現得最為不安。

由於他的幾個錯誤決定，公司的業績受到很大的影響，消息傳出去，我們的股票大跌。

如此拖了兩個月，我們這些做下屬的人都替他擔心，也替公司擔心，已經有人要跳槽。也難怪，我們過去那位極有信心的總經理好像已經完全喪失自信心了。

16-20　　又是一個週五的下午，總經理找我去。這次他又恢復了過去的表情，和我有談有笑，他給我看一瓶名貴的葡萄酒，也給我一隻極為講究的水晶酒杯，是捷克造的。然後他和我談了一些好像極有哲理的話，大意是人應該有能力控制自己的命運，如果人無法自己掌握自己的命運，活了又有什麼意義？

我卻不敢同意他的這種看法，我說我們大多數人都無法控制自己的命運，走一步是一步。比方說，一般勞工階級的人，被老闆炒魷魚者

◇ irritable（adj.）易怒的
◇ focused（adj.）專注的；心思集中的
◇ ill-advised（adj.）草率的；未經深思熟慮的
◇ dramatically（adv.）戲劇化地

◇ influence（v.）影響
◇ performance（n.）表現
◇ stock（n.）股票
◇ drag（v.）拖（此處片語 drag on，有「繼續緩慢向前」的意味，相當於 go on）

that day, he became irritable, and he often looked tired; he wasn't focused during meetings, either. The strangest thing was that he always looked the most anxious on Friday afternoons.

A few ill-advised decisions he made dramatically influenced the company's performance. As word got out, our stock fell sharply.

Things dragged on like this for two months. We employees were getting worried about him, not to mention the company—some people had already jumped ship. And you couldn't blame them—our general manager, once so self-assured, appeared to have completely lost faith in himself.

Another Friday afternoon rolled around, and the general manager asked me to see him. This time, he seemed to be his old self again: he talked and laughed with me, showed me a bottle of exceptionally fine wine and gave me an exquisite crystal wine glass from Czechoslovakia. Then he made some very philosophical-sounding remarks to the effect that a man should be able to control his own destiny, for if a man couldn't control his own destiny, what purpose was there in life?

16-20

I couldn't bring myself to agree with his point of view, however. "The vast majority of us can't control our own destinies—we live

◇ employee (n.) 職員；員工；受僱者
◇ self-assured (adj.) 胸有成竹的；自信滿滿的
◇ exquisite [ˋɛkskwɪzɪt] (adj.) 精緻的；精美的
◇ remark (n.) 話；言語
◇ destiny (n.) 命運
◇ purpose (n.) 意義
◇ majority (n.) 多數 (此處片語 the vast majority of 表示「大多數的……」)

多的很，難道他們都不該活下去不成。即使做到了總統，也可能下次選不上。我坦白地告訴他，社會上誰也無法完全掌握自己的命運。

　　他不理我，又跳到另一個話題，那就是優勝劣敗的問題，他說他仍然討厭看到智力、能力不好的人，他有一個非常可怕的想法，他認為自動化的技術會使很多這種智力平庸的人失業。對他而言，這是很自然的事。

　　我對他的言論和看法感到十分厭惡。可是又不敢和他辯論，只好告辭。可是我有一種感覺；那就是我們的總經理又恢復了他的自信心，他似乎又能掌握他的命運了。

　　當天晚上十點左右，我忽然接到一家醫院打來的電話，這家醫院的公關主任用很輕的聲音告訴我一個可怕的消息，我們的總經理自殺未遂，現在已脫離險境，因為我是公司的副總經理，他們決定告訴我。

◇ elect（v.）選舉；推選
◇ ignore（v.）忽視；不予理會
◇ chilling（adj.）令人心寒的
◇ automated technology 自動化科技（技術）

◇ mediocre [ˋmidɪͻkəʳ]（adj.）平庸的；普通的；二流的
◇ distaste（n.）厭惡
◇ confidence（n.）信心

one step at a time," I said. "For instance, lots of ordinary workers get fired by their bosses, but does that mean they shouldn't go on living? Even if you're elected president, you might not win the next election. Frankly, not a single member of society has total control over his fate."

He ignored what I said and started talking about another subject: the survival of the fittest. He still hated seeing people who lacked intelligence or talent, he said, and he expressed a chilling thought: he believed that automated technology would cause many of these mentally mediocre people to lose their jobs. In his eyes, this was a perfectly natural thing.

I felt a deep distaste for his ideas, but I didn't dare argue with him—all I could do was leave the room. But I had a feeling that our general manager had gotten his confidence back. He seemed to be in control of his destiny again.

That night at about ten, I got an unexpected call from the hospital. In a quiet voice, the public relations chief there told me some frightening news: our general manager had tried to commit suicide! Fortunately, he was now out of danger. Since I was the assistant general manager of the company, they had decided to let me know.

◇ unexpected (adj.) 料想不到的；意外的；突然的
◇ public relations chief 公關主任
◇ frightening (adj.) 嚇人的；令人害怕的
◇ assistant general manager 副總經理

21-25　　我趕到醫院，發現老張非常虛弱地躺在病床上，他的太太在旁邊，他看到了我，只說一切都好，公司的事全由我暫時看管。

　　醫院告訴我，他是由救護車送來的，有一位年輕人一直和他在一起，老張一直拉著這位年輕人的手不放。我這才發現，所謂年輕人，其實就是小李。我告訴醫生這位年輕人是我們總經理的司機，他說：「你們的總經理原來是位性情中人，他拉著司機的手，兩人好像感情很好的樣子。」

　　小李告訴我，那天總經理一直沒有下樓來，他覺得很奇怪，找了大樓的管理員，開了辦公室的門終於發現總經理伏在桌上，一隻手摸著電話機。他立刻召來救護車，陪著總經理去急救。令他大出意外的是總經理忽然拉住了他的手，即使在急救的時候，也拉他的手不放。一直到他太太趕到，他才放開。

　　我們將這個自殺的消息予以保密，否則股票又要大跌了。

◇ frail（adj.）虛弱的；無力的
◇ ambulance（n.）救護車
◇ ordeal（n.）苦難；試煉；痛苦的考驗
◇ ashamed（adj.）不好意思的；覺得丟臉的
◇ security guard 警衛（此處指大樓警衛或管理員）
◇ slumped（adj.）（無力地）癱（坐，臥）
◇ emergency room 急診室

I rushed to the hospital, where I found old Zhang lying in bed looking extremely frail, his wife at his side. When he saw me, all he said was that everything was okay, and that I would be taking charge of the company for the time being.

The hospital told me he had been brought there by ambulance in the company of a young man, whose hand he had clung to throughout the ordeal. I realized that the young man he was referring to was Little Li, the general manager's chauffeur. When I told the doctor so, he said, "Your general manager sure isn't ashamed to show his emotions. He held his chauffeur's hand like they were real close friends."

Little Li told me how the general manager never came down from his office that day. He felt that something wasn't right, so he went and got the building security guard to open his office door. They found him there, slumped over his desk, with one hand on the telephone. Little Li immediately called for an ambulance and took the general manager to the emergency room. To his amazement, all of a sudden the general manager grabbed hold of his hand and wouldn't let go, not even while he was receiving first aid. Only when his wife arrived did he finally let go.

We kept the news of his attempted suicide a secret. Otherwise, our stock would have taken another dive.

◇ grab (v.) 緊抓
◇ first aid 急救

◇ attempted suicide 自殺未遂
◇ dive (n.) (此處指股價) 下滑；下探

　　總經理終於回來上班了，他變得非常和藹可親，雖然他仍很精明，但已不再罵人，而且也會盡量說人家的好話，公司的士氣大振，業績恢復正常，而且比以前更好。

26-30　　過去總經理是不和大家吃飯的，現在他會和大家一起吃午飯，有時和同事一起到門口麵店去吃擔仔麵。過去，他從不關懷同仁，現在，同仁有什麼煩惱，他會表示關心，而且我感覺到關心並不是假的。

　　可是我知道他自殺過，而且自殺前曾有過明顯的不安，他究竟怕什麼呢？

　　我想起了被他開除的老陳，莫非老陳真的每週五都去嚇唬他？老陳在另一家電子公司做事，我打電話去問他有沒有做這種事。老陳呼天搶地地大呼冤枉，他說他第二天就找到了事，薪水也加了。根本就把總經理忘得一乾二淨，從來就沒有去找過他，當時他只是亂講的。

◇ brilliance（n.）光彩
◇ amiable [ˋemɪəbḷ]（adj.）和氣的
◇ approachable（adj.）可親近的
◇ morale [məˋræl]（n.）士氣
◇ soar（v.）高飛；高漲
◇ danzai noodles 擔仔麵（由中文音譯而來，台灣民間麵食小吃，起源於台南）

◇ noodle parlor 麵店；麵攤
◇ colleague [ˋkɑlig]（n.）同事
◇ concern（n.）關懷
◇ genuine（adj.）真正的；真心的
◇ visible（adj.）可看得到的
◇ anxiety（n.）憂慮
◇ recall（v.）回想起；憶起

Eventually, the general manager came back to work. Although he had lost none of his brilliance, he had become amiable and approachable: he no longer yelled at people, and he tried to speak highly of others. Morale soared, and our business recovered—we were doing better than ever.

The boss never used to eat with the rest of us, but now he'd have lunch with everyone, and sometimes he'd go out with a few coworkers for danzai noodles at the noodle parlor by the building entrance. He never used to care about his colleagues, but now he expressed concern whenever they had problems, and I could feel that his concern was genuine.

26-30

But I knew he had tried to kill himself, and he'd gone through a period of visible anxiety before that. So what had he been afraid of?

I recalled Old Chen, the fellow he had fired. Was it possible that he'd actually gone to frighten his old boss every Friday? Old Chen was currently working at another electronics company; I gave him a call and asked if he had done such a thing. Old Chen vehemently denied my accusation. He said that he'd found a new job with a better income the day after he was fired. He'd completely forgotten about our general manager—he never once went looking for him. What he'd said that afternoon was just an empty threat.

◇ currently(adv.)現時地；目前；當下
◇ vehemently ['viəməntlı](adv.)強烈地；激烈地
◇ accusation(n.)指控；控訴
◇ threat(n.)威脅

又過了一陣子，老陳忽然興奮得不得了，說有東西要給我看，我們約好在一家咖啡廳見面，他給我一封信，信是總經理寄給他的。全文如下：

陳兄：

31-35

我要在這裡謝謝你，因為你改變了我的一生。

打從高中起，我就發現我天賦很好，而且我也很討厭那些平庸的人，我的確相信優勝劣敗、物競天擇的道理。

可是我也一直非常害怕，因為我怕萬一我的天賦出了毛病，怎麼辦？比方說，萬一我出了車禍，得了腦震盪，記憶力和判斷力都衰退了，我豈不應該被淘汰出局？

雖然我有這種憂慮，卻一直不嚴重，只是偶爾會有這種想法而已。可是那天你說每個週五都會來找我，我就每個週五晚上都會作噩夢。夢裡我變成了一個能力十分平庸的人。

◇ arrange (v.) 安排
◇ entirety (n.) 整體；全部
◇ gifted (adj.) 有天份的；有才氣的
◇ thoroughly ['θɜolɪ] (adv.) 完全地；徹頭徹尾地

◇ suffer (v.) 遭受
◇ concussion [kən'kʌʃən] (n.) 衝擊（此處指「腦震盪」）
◇ analytical ability [ˌænl'ɪtɪkl̩] 分析能力
◇ prospect (n.) 未來可能發生的事

Time continued to pass until one day, out of the blue, a very excited Old Chen told me he had something he wanted to show me. We arranged to meet at a coffee shop. He handed me a letter our general manager had sent him. It read, in its entirety, as follows:

Dear Old Chen,

I want to take this opportunity to thank you for changing my life. 31-35

Round about the time I was in high school, I realized I was very gifted, and I started to dislike ordinary people. I thoroughly believed in natural selection and the survival of the fittest.

But I was also constantly afraid, afraid of what would happen if something ever went wrong with my talents. For instance, if I were in a car accident and suffered a concussion that ruined my memory and analytical ability, wouldn't I be "weeded out"?

Although I suffered some anxiety over the prospect, it wasn't too serious—thoughts like that occurred to me only occasionally. But after that day when you said you'd come looking for me every Friday, I started having nightmares every Friday night. In the nightmares, I would become a person of very mediocre talents.

◇ occasionally (adv.) 偶爾；時或　　　◇ nightmare (n.) 夢魘

舉例來說，我第一個夢是我又回到了高中時代，老師叫我們跳木馬，我卻不會跳，怎麼樣都跳不過去，丟臉之至。

36-40　　第二個夢是我參加聯招，結果是幾乎一題也答不出來，急得一身冷汗，醒來以後也真是渾身汗濕了。

問題是：每一個週五，我必定會作這種夢，夢裡我永遠是窩囊到極點。有一次夢到公司的產品完全設計錯了，被客戶大批退貨。

由於每個週五晚上都要被折磨一個晚上，我開始怕週五，整個星期，我真的生活在恐懼之中。我知道我正慢慢失去控制我命運的能力。因此我決定自殺，因為只有這樣，我可以證明我仍有控制命運的能力。

可是安眠藥使我昏沉下去的時候，不知何故，我腦子卻極為清醒，我極想活下去。我忽然想通了，能力不好又有什麼關係，人只要活得快樂，即使沒有出人頭地，不也是很好嗎？我想起了我

◇ gym class 體育課
◇ vault (v.)（以竿或手支撐）騰空而跳
◇ entrance exam 入學考試
◇ cold sweat 冷汗
◇ soaked (adj.) 濕透的

◇ incompetent (adj.) 無能的；能力不足的
◇ product (n.) 產品
◇ customer (n.) 客戶；顧客
◇ torture (n.) 折磨；痛苦
◇ dread (v.) 害怕；畏懼

For example, in my first nightmare, I was back in high school gym class. The teacher had asked our class to vault over the horse, but no matter how hard I tried, I couldn't jump over it. I felt so ashamed!

36-40

In the second nightmare, I was taking the national college entrance exam. As I took the test, I almost couldn't answer a single question. I was so anxious that I broke out in a cold sweat. When I woke up, my whole body was soaked.

The problem was that I had the nightmares every single Friday, and in every one of them I was totally incompetent. Once I dreamed that all our company's products had been designed wrong, and all our customers returned them.

Since each Friday night was torture to me, I started dreading Fridays. All through the week I lived in fearful apprehension. I knew I was slowly losing the ability to control my own destiny. That's why I decided to kill myself—it was the only way I could prove that I was still in control.

But just as my body was succumbing to the sleeping pills, somehow my mind felt very awake, and I desperately wanted to go on living. Then a flash of inspiration came to me: what did it matter if I had no remarkable talents? As long as a man is happy

◇ apprehension (n.) 憂心；疑懼
◇ succumb (to) [sə`kʌm] (v.) 屈從；臣服
◇ desperately (adv.) 絕望地；拼命地

◇ inspiration (n.) 靈感
◇ remarkable (adj.) 不凡的

　　的司機小李，在我快死之前，我很想大聲地告訴他，我羨慕你，因為你老是快快樂樂地，可是我已沒有力氣了，我的手碰到了電話機，但無法打電話。

　　當小李破門而入的時候，我高興極了，我設法拉住他的手，無非是要告訴他，我是個非常普通的人，我要人可憐我，我再也不敢講優勝劣敗了。

41-44　　我現在活得快樂多了，我已完全沒有過去的那種恐懼，因為我知道做個普通人乃是正常的事。即使我不如人家，我也不再太介意了。

　　這一切都該謝謝你，是你使我每週五都作噩夢，是你使我自殺，也虧得我做了這件傻事，我才發現我根本就是個普通的人。

張××

◇ prominence（n.）卓越；傑出
◇ verge（n.）邊緣（此處片語 on the verge of ，表示「瀕臨……」或「快要……」）
◇ envy（v.）羨慕
◇ overjoyed（adj.）非常高興的

with his life, even if he doesn't achieve prominence, isn't he still perfectly well off? I thought of my chauffeur, Little Li. As I sat there on the verge of death, I really wanted to tell him how much I envied him for always being so happy. But I had no strength left. My hand touched the telephone, but I couldn't make a call.

When Little Li broke through the door, I was overjoyed. I found the strength to hold his hand for one simple reason: I wanted to tell him what an ordinary person I was. I needed sympathy. I no longer dared to advocate the survival of the fittest.

Now my life is much happier than it was before. I no longer have the fear I once did because I know that it's normal to be an ordinary person. Even if I'm not as gifted as others, I honestly don't mind anymore.   **41-44**

I have you to thank for all of this. It was you who made me have nightmares each Friday; it was you who made me try to kill myself; and it was because I tried to do such a stupid thing that I finally realized I'm nothing but an ordinary man.

Zhang _____

◇ advocate (v.) 主張；鼓吹；倡言
◇ normal (adj.) 正常的

◇ honestly [ˈɑnɪstlɪ] (adv.) 說實在地；說真格地

　　我們兩人都啞然失笑，我們向來體育也不好，書也念不好，因此實在無法想像會有這種事。不會跳木馬，考試考不好，家常便飯也。沒有才能的人，是不會怕失去才能的。我們從不會羨慕那些能幹得不得了的人，他們其實都生活在恐懼之中。我們不過分強調優勝劣敗，所以對失敗沒有如此的害怕。

　　總經理現在和他的司機有談有笑，今天我看到他拖小李去吃臭豆腐。小李一臉苦相，顯然不喜歡吃臭豆腐，他一定後悔當年救了總經理一命。

◇ sensation（n.）感覺
◇ familiar（adj.）熟悉的；親切的
◇ competent（adj.）能力強的
◇ emphasize（v.）重視；強調；看重

The two of us couldn't help laughing in spite of ourselves. We had never been good at gym, nor were we ever brilliant students, so it was impossible for us to imagine the terror Old Zhang felt when faced with those prospects. To us, the sensation of not being able to vault over a horse in gym or doing poorly on a test was as familiar as the taste of home cooking. The non-gifted have no need to worry about losing their gifts. We had never envied the extremely competent, for they live in a constant state of fear. We had never overly emphasized the survival of the fittest, so failure had never been such a frightening thing to us.

Now our boss and his chauffeur talk and laugh together. Today I saw him drag Little Li off to eat stinky tofu. From the pained expression on Little Li's face, it was easy to see that he was not a stinky tofu fan. No doubt he regretted having saved his boss's life.

◇ drag (v.) 硬拉；強拖
◇ stinky tofu 臭豆腐

◇ pained (adj.) 痛苦的
◇ regret (v.) 後悔

（1）admire somebody for something 因某事而崇敬某人（1段）

Everyone who knew General Manager Zhang admired him for his talents.

所有認識張總經理的人都佩服他的才能。

解析

這個片語和各位在國中所學過的 thank someone for something 異曲同工。只要把 thank someone for something 其中的 thank 替換成 admire，不就是了嗎？讀者唯一要做的事是，把 admire 這個單字背起來，本書譯者郝凱揚先生不是曾提醒讀者：學習英文，要特別注意動詞的用法嗎？所以，讀者們，注意了，admire 的意思是「欽佩」、「崇拜」、「景仰」，而常用在 admire someone for something 這樣的形式裡。

小試身手

1. 他是個有原則的人，而人們也因為這一點而崇敬他。

_____

（2）no matter what 無論什麼；凡是什麼（1段）

No matter what it was that he wanted to learn how to do, he'd learn to do it exceptionally well.

凡是他想學的他都會學得非常好。

解析

no matter 之後可以跟著很多以 wh~ 起頭的疑問詞，no matter（who, what, which, when, where, why, how），理論是如此，可是眼尖的讀者應該可以察覺到，no matter why 絕少在閱讀中出現，no matter what reason 倒是有可

能。這種子句，在文法上名之為「讓步副詞子句」，為什麼叫作「讓步」，讀者其實可以不用深究，把它當成是文法上的一個術語即可，就如你聽到「時間」副詞子句或「地方」副詞子句一樣。副詞子句一般用於修飾主要子句，尤其是主要子句的動詞部分。這裡的讓步副詞子句：No matter what it was that he wanted to learn how to do 就是用來修飾主要子句：he'd learn to do it exceptionally well。

本句另外有個重點：exceptionally well。exception 是名詞，原本是「例外」的意思，因此把副詞形式 exceptionally 和 well 放在一起，當然就是「格外地好」、「好的出奇」。

小試身手

2.　無論人們怎麼說他，他就是笑笑而不予理會。

＿＿＿＿＿＿＿＿＿＿＿＿＿＿＿＿＿＿＿＿＿＿＿＿

---

(3) not only... but... as well 不只……而且……（2段）

For example, in middle school, he was not only an outstanding student but an outstanding athlete as well...

舉例來說，在中學的時候他不僅功課非常好，連體育都非常好……

解析

多數讀者都記得一個牢不可破的片語 not only... but also...，這裡的 not only... but... as well 不如就把它當成是個突變體吧。其實 as well 本就具有「也（also）」的意思，用它來取代標準式的 also 合情合理，只要記得把它的位置挪到後面去就是了。另外，形容詞 outstanding 是「拔尖的」、「出色的」、「傑出的」之意，因此 an outstanding student 為「傑出的學生」、「功課一把罩」，而 an outstanding athlete 為「出色的運動員」、「運動好手」。

小試身手

3. 如果人口增加不予以控制，不只會傷害一個國家的經濟發展，而且會引發其他嚴重的社會問題。

_____

（4）（be）a cut above the rest 勝人一籌；出類拔萃（2段）

Even after getting into the electrical engineering department of National Taiwan University, he was still a cut above the rest.

進了台大念電機系以後，他仍然是出人頭地。

解析

在此不妨把 cut 當作是量杯上的一個「刻度」，現在這個刻度（cut）高過（above）其他的刻度（the rest），試問這不就是中文所謂的「勝過一籌」？

小試身手

4. 他（原）就讀機械工程系，但在念完大一後轉到電機系。

_____

（5）have one's hands full 忙碌不堪；忙得不可開交（2段）

Most of his classmates were so busy that they had their hands full just trying to pass their exams...

大多數同學應付考試都來不及。

解析

手捧著剛修好的電腦，走在校園的步道上，迎面來了個校園美女，手上捧著一疊書，一個不平衡，掉下了兩本，美女向著你看過來，希望你能想想辦

法、幫幫忙，She hopes you can give her a hand. ——你當然想幫忙，可是自己手上一個沉甸甸的電腦，實在心有餘而力不足，只好給她一個歉意的微笑，說 I'd love to help, but as you can see, I have my hands full. 所以，這句話常用以指有要務纏身，分身不得，難以幫上他人的忙。

解析

> **小試身手**
>
> 5. 我本來打算請她幫忙的，但是她忙得分不開身(忙得不可開交)。
>
> _____

(6) start out as... 從擔任……開始；以……起家(3段)

He started out as an ordinary engineer but quickly rose to become the general manager of our company.

(他)從普通的工程師做起，一帆風順地做到了我們公司的總經理。

解析

很好的一個片語，剛踏出校門，無論專業或經驗，都有待琢磨歷練，一切都得從頭開始，由基層作起。這個片語就剛好表示「從(某)職務開始」，介詞 as 的後面常跟著一個表示某職位的名詞。人生路途，從生嫩到圓熟，有一定的歷程，有必經的階段，不要以剛開始的職位卑微為意，只要不要眼高手低 (Never set a goal higher than you can reach.)，終究不至於一事無成吧！

> **小試身手**
>
> 6. 這是人盡皆知的故事，那位企業大亨由送米的夥計做起。
>
> _____

(7) be utterly devoid of（sympathy）完全沒有（同情心）（4段）

We all admired him, but not one of us liked him, for General Manager Zhang was utterly devoid of sympathy.

我們大家都佩服他，可是我們都全體一致地討厭他，因為張總經理是完全沒有什麼同情心的人。

解析

如果告訴你，要學會 be devoid of 這個片語，可以從 be full of 出發，你同意嗎？話講到這裡，相信有些反應快的讀者已經意會過來了。的確，full 是「充實」、「飽滿」的意思，be full of... 當然就是「充滿著……」的意思。把 full 抽掉，換上 devoid，這個 devoid 是「空泛」、「虛無」的意思，那麼 be devoid of... 豈不就表達了「沒有……」、「不具……」的意思了嗎？ devoid 之前加了個副詞 utterly，把 devoid「虛」、「空」的程度再往上提昇了一步，表示出相當於中文的「全然沒有」、「毫不具備」的意思。現在讓我們反過來看 be full of...，如果也想提昇 full「飽」、「滿」的程度，怎麼做呢？把它放在小試身手好了。

小試身手

7. 箱子裡滿滿都是雜七雜八的小東西。

_____

(8) have（absolutely）no reservations about...（做某事）毫不保留；（做某事）無所顧忌（4段）

He had absolutely no reservations about expressing his contempt for anyone of inferior ability.

對於任何能力差的人，他一概毫不保留地表示他的輕視。

解析

投宿旅店，櫃台人員一般會問上一句「有訂房嗎？」對應的英文為：Do you have a reservation? 可見 reservation 為「預訂」、「預留」、「預約」之意。因此，have no reservations about... 可想而知，就表達了「對……無所保留」、「不吝於……」的意思。在之前加個副詞，為的是把否定的味道更徹底強化，表示「絕沒有」、「毫無」的意思。contempt 意為「輕蔑」、「瞧不起」，所以，express（show）his contempt for someone 即是「蔑視某人」、「瞧不起某人」的意思。

小試身手

8. 他一點都不保留地讓大眾知道他的不滿。

_____

(9) it is self-evident that...（某事）明顯不過；（某事）本該如此（4段）

To him, it was self-evident that untalented people ought to step aside and let the more capable take the reins of society.

（對他來說，在他看來）能力差的人絕對應該讓路，使能力高的人能夠掌握社會。

解析

來作個拆字遊戲，把 self-evident 拆成 self 和 evident 兩部分（註：其實它本來就是這兩部分所構成的複合字）。self 為「自己」、「本身」，而 evident 則為「顯而易見」、「昭然若揭」。所以，這個複合字當然就是「本身就很清楚明白，無庸贅言」的意思。其次，英文有一個現象，即定冠詞後面接某些形容詞，其效果相當於複數名詞 (the adj. = adj. Ns)。讀者可以看到，英

譯裡的 the more capable 其實就相當於 more capable people 或 people of greater capability。最後請注意 take the reins of(society)，reins 為操控馬行動的韁繩，因此 take the reins of 即是「操控」、「駕馭」的意思。

小試身手

9. 這還用說，他是在以卵擊石。

_____

（10）meet someone in person 會見本人（5段）
　　　（someone）be handicapped（某人）肢體殘障；行動不便

But when he met him in person, he discovered that Old Wang was handicapped: he had to walk with a cane.

可是他和老王見面以後，才發現老王是位殘障人士，走路必須用拐杖。

解析

meet someone in person 指的是「會見某人本尊」。handicapped 為形容詞，指「肢體殘障的」、「生理有缺陷的」，造句時，一般會在前面置 BE 動詞，請看以下的句子：I know he is slightly handicapped, for he doesn't walk naturally.

小試身手

10-1. 任何想和她親自見面的人都被要求事先預約。

_____

10-2. 應該設置更多的殘障專用廁所。

_____

（11）strike up a（casual）conversation with... 和（某人）（閒）聊起來（6段）

Little Li had been his chauffeur for six and a half years, but the boss had never once struck up a casual conversation with him, not even on a two-hour car ride.

小李是他的司機，替他開了六年半的車，他從來沒和他談過一句閒話，即使兩小時的車程，他也不會和他談一句話。

解析

動詞 strike 具有「演奏（樂器、樂曲）」的意思，所以片語 strike up 就具備了「開始演奏」的意味。strike（up）a tune 表示「開始彈奏一首曲子」，現在把 a tune 替換成 a conversation，不就表示「開始進行一段對談」嗎？本片語也寫成 begin（start）a conversation with...。

小試身手

11. 通常我會主動和坐在我隔壁的乘客攀談。

_____

（12）excel academically 成績優異；功課良好（7段）

Back then, most high school students who excelled academically were lousy at gym, while the athletic guys tended to be dumb jocks.

（在那個時候）大多數高中生功課好的話，體育就奇差，體育好的傢伙卻大多只是四肢發達、頭腦簡單。

解析

學英文學到好像也有些程度了，可是有時旁人問到一些很家常、很普通的日常語句，猛然之間，還真覺得不是那麼容易表達，或者也沒有把握是對是錯。這裡就是個例子：簡簡單單三個字「功課好」，可能就要令多數讀者

楞在當場。對照英譯一看,原來是 excel academically,輕描淡寫,道地無比。在本句我們尚可學到 lousy at gym 和 dumb jock。前者指的是「體育奇差」,後者是中文習稱的「頭腦簡單、四肢發達的人」。dumb 本意是「笨拙」、「不靈光」,而 jock 本意為「賽馬騎師」,在美國俚語裡面引申為「壯漢」。

小試身手

12. 雖然那個名人在事業上非常成功,但他有很多家庭的問題。

_____

---

(13) a man of average ability 平庸之輩;才具普通的人(8段)

Old Chen was a man of average ability, but he was a hard worker, and since diligence can compensate for clumsiness, he had always performed pretty well.

老陳才能中等,可是做事十分認真,因為勤能補拙,他的表現還不錯。

解析

形容詞 average 的本意是「平均的」,因而也就衍生出「中庸的」、「普通的」、「平庸的」的意思。所以 a man of average ability 當然就是指「才具平庸之輩」。如果是「大才大能之輩」那自然就用 a man of great ability 來表達。這種 a man(person)of... 的表示法讀者一定要花些時間去適應熟悉。我們多提供幾個讓讀者練習(參考答案置於小試身手解答裡):

有原則的人:_____

有學問的人(飽學之士):_____

有德之人:_____

有財之人(富人):_____

另外，英譯裡有個很重要的片語 compensate for，其意思為「彌補」、「補償」。剛好原著裡有句中文格言：「勤能補拙」，因此讀者也就看到了很好的英譯：Diligence can compensate for clumsiness.

小試身手

13. 沒有什麼能讓有強烈決心的人受挫。

_____

(14) make up for lost time 彌補損失的時間（8段）

...but now that she had passed away, he felt sure he could make up for lost time and get caught up on his work.

……他母親已去世，他應該可以彌補過去的時間，將進度趕上。

解析

很難得，也很湊巧，make up 和 catch up 兩個片語，竟然同時出現在同一個英譯句裡。make up 的本意是將還欠缺的、還不完整的「補起來」，而 catch up 指的是把落後的「趕上來」、從後面「追上來」。當然請讀者進一步留意這兩個片語後面所接的介詞：make up for 和 catch up on，順便提醒讀者，catch up with 也有可能，如果指的是「追趕上某人」。

小試身手

14. 請了兩個星期的病假後，我不知道要怎麼彌補沒上的課。功課要趕上其他同學會很難。

_____

（15）upon... 在……之際（9段）

Anyone else would have shown a little sympathy upon learning that Old Chen's mother had passed away...

別人一聽到老陳的母親去世，都會稍微表示一點同情之意。

解析

這是介詞 upon 的獨門用法，讀者需要用心體會。在這個用法裡，upon 表示「一……就……」的味道。小孩子「一」聽到門鈴響「就」衝去開門 (Upon hearing the bell ring, the kids rushed to open the door.)；學生們「一」聽到老師宣布小考「就」唉聲連連 (Upon hearing the teacher announce a quiz, the students began to groan.)。

另外，本句還有兩個需要花些時間學習的東西，一個是 show(no, a little, a lot of)sympathy，意思為「對……表示（不，稍稍，非常）同情」，有時候後面接介詞 for 或 towards 以表示對（某人）同情。另一個為 pass away，意思為「去世」、「過世」，是死亡 (die) 的委婉說法。

小試身手

15. 一聽到消息，吉姆就高興得跳了起來。

_____

（16）do poor work 表現不佳（9段）
　　　get the hell out 滾開
　　　fall behind in（its）work 工作進度落後

He said that anyone who did poor work for any reason should get the hell out, because the company loses a lot of money when it falls behind in its work.

他說任何人表現不好，就應該滾蛋，不論什麼理由，因為公司的工作進

度落後，損失很大。

解析

和重點十二「功課良好」如出一轍，我們又遇到了「表現不佳」和「進度落後」這類生活用語，且又是有口難言。請讀者再回到本重點開頭處，把三個用語用心看過，你會更有心得。當然你若之前學過（表現不佳：do a lousy job）、（滾開；滾蛋：quit 或 step aside）、（工作進度落後：cannot meet the job requirements）之類的用語，也可交替運用。在此要注意 get the hell out 是語氣粗魯的說法。

小試身手

16. 我知道我沒有班上同學聰明，所以我要很努力才不會進度落後。

_____

(17)（be）a great blow to... 對……（是）一大打擊（10段）

...being fired like this was obviously a great blow to him.
……這個被開除的打擊對他當然很大。

解析

blow 為「打擊」，因此 a great blow 就是「重大打擊」，而 a heavy blow 即是「沉重打擊」，完整的片語 (be)a great blow to someone 就是「對某人的重大打擊」。

在本句裡的 fire 為「開除」、「革職」之意，being fired 為被動（be Vpp），表示成 being fired（動名詞形）乃是因為它在句子裡居主詞的地位（動詞為 was），既然是主詞，總不能寫成 be fired 吧。

小試身手

17. 又損失一艘船帶給他和他的事業一個沉重打擊。

_____

（18）plead for mercy with someone 向（某人）求情（10段）

Then, probably because he knew it was useless to plead for mercy with someone like General Manager Zhang, he left without a word.

大概他也知道對張總經理這種人，懇求他開恩是做不到，所以他就一言不發地離開了。

解析

要學會這個片語，讀者們得先記住 plead for mercy 是「求情」、「請求開恩」的意思。之後再添個 with someone 就成了「向某人求情」、「請某人開恩」的意思。也可把動詞改成 ask for「請求」或 beg for「乞求」。此處還有兩個重點，一個是 it is useless... ；另一個為 without(saying)a word。前者表示「做某事徒然無益」，比如「和他講道理徒然無益」，以英文表示則為：It is useless to reason with him. 而後者則表示「不發一語」、「一聲不吭」的意思，比如「他坐下來，一聲不吭地用遙控器把電視打開。」以上這句就放在小試身手裡，給你一個機會大展身手。

小試身手

18-1. 我懇求開恩，可是他並不給情面。

_____

18-2. 他坐下來，一聲不吭地用遙控器把電視打開。

_____

（19）a trace of alarm 一絲／抹／驚恐（的神情）（12段）

I didn't understand what Old Chen meant by what he said, but I noticed a trace of alarm on General Manager Zhang's face.

我也不懂老陳的話什麼意思，可是我注意到我們的張總經理臉上露出了一絲恐懼的表情。

解析

先從 alarm 說起，作名詞解時，意思為「警報」、「驚恐」；作動詞解則為「使心生警覺」、「使心生惶恐」之意。另一個和 alarm 有關的字為 alarmed，為形容詞，指「惶恐的」、「驚惶不安的」的心理狀態。在本重點裡，alarm 是名詞，因此 a trace of alarm 就是指「一絲的驚恐」之意。trace 本身表示「微量」之意，因此 a trace of... 相當於中文的「一絲的……」、「一丁點的……」。

小試身手

19. 他臉上看不出一丁點悔不當初的樣子。

＿＿＿＿＿＿＿＿＿＿＿＿＿＿＿＿＿＿＿＿＿＿＿＿

（20）just blow smoke 只是虛張聲勢（12段）

Mild-mannered Old Chen was just blowing smoke—there was nothing to fear.

溫和的老陳一定是說說而已，有什麼好怕的。

解析

只是「（氣得）冒煙」just blow smoke，又不是真的「失火」set(something) on fire 或「冒火」flare up，有什麼好緊張的呢？有些人一時情緒失控，說兩句狠話，摔兩個杯子，只是發洩一下胸中怒氣（He is just venting.），虛張聲勢一下（He is just bluffing.），這時候也不必太當真或太過緊張，當事人個性

温和 mild-mannered，不會出什麼大亂子的。

小試身手

20. 學生們以為老師只是虛張聲勢。他們所不知道的是這次他真的大
發脾氣了。

_____

---

(21) word got out 消息傳出 (14段)

As word got out, our stock fell sharply.
消息傳出去，我們的股票大跌。

解析

word got out 是典型的慣用語，想要學會，只有死記一途，別無他法。word
在這裡當「消息」、「傳言」，至於 get out 兩字，從字面看就很清楚了。股價
(stock price)「猛然下挫」、「急遽下跌」，譯者以 fell sharply 來處理。當然
你也可以使用 plummeted 來表示。

小試身手

21. 消息一出，他的社會形象 (public image) 受到了相當大的毀損。

_____

---

(22) things drag on like this 事情就這樣拖下去 (15段)

Things dragged on like this for two months.
如此拖了兩個月。

解析

動詞 drag 的意思不但是「拖」,而且是很沉重地、很費力氣地「拖」,特別注意 on 在這裡其實並非是一般認為的「介詞」,而是「副詞」,但是因為它是介詞轉任的副詞,所以就文法言,它被稱為「介副詞」,請記得,這種用法的 on 具有「繼續」的傾向。所以 Things dragged on. 為「事情繼續拖(下去)」,Things dragged on like this. 為「事情就這樣子繼續拖(下去)」,演變到最後 Things dragged on like this for two months. 當然就是「事情就這樣子繼續拖了兩個月」。

小試身手

22. 事情就這樣拖下去,沒有改善也沒有惡化,直到沒有人再提起。

_____

(23) not to mention... 更不用說……(15段)

We employees were getting worried about him, not to mention the company—some people had already jumped ship.

我們這些做下屬的人都替他擔心,也替公司擔心,已經有人要跳槽。

解析

這個口語用在什麼場合呢?請看以下兩個例子。

◇ 他長於潛水,游泳就更不在話下了。
He's good at diving, not to mention swimming.

◇ 他埃弗勒斯峰都攀登過了,玉山就更別提了。
He conquered Mt. Everest, not to mention Mt. Jade.

所以,這片語是用在,大風大浪都見識過了,怎會在乎小小漣漪;五湖四海都遊過了,怎會把淺溪窄河放在眼裡。所以「某某人南極都去過了,那長城就更不用說了。」這種話有點誇張,也未必切合實際,說不定有人偏就去過

南極而沒到過長城。不過，這就是人話，人講話難免有誇張的時候，不是嗎？

小試身手

23. 他南極都去過了，那長城就更不用說了。

_____

---

(24)(be)one's old self again 又回復到老樣子(16段)

This time, he seemed to be his old self again: he talked and laughed with me...

這次他又恢復了過去的表情，和我有談有笑……

解析

你想過人生，想過自己嗎？現在的自己和過去的自己有什麼不同呢？未來的自己和現在的自己又會一致嗎？人生充滿了變數，可能變好，也可能變壞。一個人變回到過去的自我 to be one's old self，可能是進步，也可能是墮落。所以本解析重點 (be)one's old self again 意思上就相當中文的「回復某人舊有本色」。英文有這種說法：He's not himself today. 表示他今天狀況（心理上的、生理上的）不穩定，和平日不同，和他接觸要謹慎小心。

小試身手

24. 我們都很高興他又回到過去的老樣子(恢復正常)。

_____

(25) to the effect that... 大意是……（16段）

Then he made some very philosophical-sounding remarks to the effect that a man should be able to control his own destiny...

然後他和我談了一些好像極有哲理的話，大意是人應該有能力控制自己的命運……

解析

這個片語的難度較高，在閱讀中碰到可能要苦思半天，才反應得過來，當然前提是要記過學過。核心字眼是 effect：「主旨」、「大意」。that 是連接詞，後面接著名詞子句。

本重點另一個值得一學的東西是 make(some)remarks，指的是「講了一些話」、「發表一些言論」。

小試身手

25. 她信裡的大意是她不克赴約。

＿＿＿＿＿＿＿＿＿＿＿＿＿＿＿＿

(26) the vast majority of... 絕大多數的……（17段）

The vast majority of us can't control our own destinies...

我們大多數人都無法控制自己的命運。

解析

majority 和 minority 是兩個相對的字，前者意為「多數」，而後者意為「少數」。因此，vast majority 當然就是「絕大多數」的意思，和 a very large portion of..., a high percentage of... 等片語意思相去不遠，都在著重高比例的「多」。

小試身手

26. 在場大多數人都贊成再興建一所醫療中心。

_____

(27) in one's eyes 在（某人）看來；在（某人）眼中(18段)

In his eyes, this was a perfectly natural thing.
對他而言，這是很自然的事。

解析

這是一個明白易懂，卻又重要實用的用語，直接從字面就可以看出「在某人眼中」的意思來，可是讀者不妨加以引申，「依（某人）看來」、「從（某人）的角度看」，甚至如本文「對（某人）而言」。

本句有個很實用的副詞 perfectly，常被用來加強形容詞的程度，語意相當於中文的「極其」。比如，你贊同某人的看法正確，而且正確極了，你就可以說：You're perfectly right. 此話一出，對方不感動也難。

小試身手

27. 在他們看來，持之以恆是學習新語言成功最重要的因素。

_____

(28) feel a deep distaste for... 對……深惡痛絕(19段)

I felt a deep distaste for his ideas, but I didn't dare argue with him—all I could do was leave the room.
我對他的言論和看法感到十分厭惡。可是又不敢和他辯論，只好告辭。

解析

taste 除了一般當「味道」解釋，也有「愛好」、「嗜好」的意思，如此一來，distaste 是「嫌惡」、「厭膩」的意思就十分清楚了。表示「對某事有一份愛好」即為 feel/ have a taste for...；「對某事有一份嫌厭」就是 feel/ have a distaste for...。

除了用 deep 來表示「深切的」來強化「嫌厭」的程度，類似的形容詞都可以派得上用場，比如也可以說 feel a strong distaste for 或者 feel an intense distaste for。甚至再進一步把形容詞改為 unspeakable，把 distaste 改為 dislike，讓整個片語變成 feel an unspeakable dislike for... 都在表達「厭惡得不得了」的意思。

小試身手

28. 我們都很討厭他說話誇張。

_____

(29) commit suicide 自殺（20段）

In a quiet voice, the public relations chief there told me some frightening news: our general manager had tried to commit suicide!

這家醫院的公關主任用很輕的聲音告訴我一個可怕的消息，我們的總經理自殺未遂。

解析

commit 真是個晦澀的字眼，定義很難真確掌握，用法更是繁複，很不好用。這就是為什麼要將它列為重點的原因。講到「殺人」，多數讀者會聯想到 kill somebody；講到「被殺（害）」，多數讀者會聯想到 be/ get killed；那麼「自殺」呢？多數讀者會聯想到 kill oneself。會聯想到 commit suicide 應該是少數吧！所以，多看它幾眼吧。這裡的 commit 是「犯（罪）」的意思，如 committing a crime，自殺也被視為罪行之一，所以也用 commit。

29. 這個免費熱線目的在預防人們自殺。

_____

(30) for the time being 暫時(21段)

When he saw me, all he said was that everything was okay, and that I would be taking charge of the company for the time being.

他看到了我,只說一切都好,公司的事全由我暫時看管。

解析

這也是個折煞人的片語,四個字都很簡單,要命的是,這四個字放在一起,到底是什麼呢?唉,沒辦法,這就是英文。其實中文不也如此,「杯」、「弓」、「蛇」、「影」四個簡單的字組合成「杯弓蛇影」,也不見得每個以中文為母語的人都知道。

話說回來,要認識 for the time being,讀者不妨想想以下如 for two hours, for three days, for a(long)while, for a year 這幾個時間副詞片語的意思。如果沒問題,for the time being 是什麼意思也就呼之欲出了。介詞 for 指的是「一段持續的時間」,the time being 則是「當下現前的時間」,那麼 for the time being 豈不就是「當下持續的這段時間」,不就是「目前暫時」的意思嗎?

另外,片語 take(full)charge of...,指的是「負(全)責」、「(全權)掌控/管」這方面的意思。

30. 目前我暫不考慮移民外國。

_____

(31) in the company of somebody 由某人相陪(22段)

The hospital told me he had been brought there by ambulance in the company of a young man, whose hand he had clung to throughout the ordeal.

醫院告訴我，他是由救護車送來的，有一位年輕人一直和他在一起，老張一直拉著這位年輕人的手不放。

【解析】

這個重點不只 in the company of...，讀者還要注意兩個重要的東西，一個是 whose 的用法，另一個為 cling to 這個片語。

先從 in the company of 說起，特別注意，本文之前也出現 company 這個字，當「公司」解釋，但在此處，company 卻是當「相隨」、「作陪」解，因此 in the company of somebody 即是「由某人陪同」的意思。

再來談 whose 這個字，它是關係代名詞，是 who 的所有格，用在關係子句需要所有格的時候。以下有個題目，目的是讓你熟悉和區別，二選一，你有百分之百的機會（如果你關係代名詞的觀念正確），至少你也有百分之五十的機會（如果你關係代名詞的觀念不正確的話）。

Bill's father, (who, whose) invention won the top prize, had never received any regular schooling.

Bill's father, (who, whose) taught us lessons in astronomy, graduated from Harvard.

最後來看看 cling to 這個片語。它是「緊緊抓／跟／黏／攀著不棄不放」，表示兩者間的關係，無論有形無形，緊密難分。比如「雖然我已經長大了，還是對媽媽依戀很深。」就可以表達為：Though I'm a grown-up, I cling to my mother emotionally all the same.

31. 他被(人)看到在兩位助理伴隨下進入該建築物。

_____

(32) to one's amazement 令某人驚奇(23)

To his amazement, all of a sudden the general manager grabbed hold of his hand and wouldn't let go, not even while he was receiving first aid.

令他大出意外的是總經理忽然拉住了他的手,即使在急救時,也拉他的手不放。

解析

「to one's + 強烈情緒」是重點,意思相當於中文「令某某人產生某種感覺」。中文有「喜怒哀樂」之類的情緒,「令我大喜」、「令他大怒」、「讓老媽哀傷」、「令老師大樂」,以上如果用英文表示,分別為 to my great joy, much to his annoyance, to my mother's(deep)grief, to the teacher's amusement/ delight。

另外兩個片語:all of a sudden 和 grabbed hold of...。前者指「猛然」、「突然間」。後者則如中文「一把(牢牢地)抓住」。這也請背起來。

32. 很令我痛苦的是,我姊姊還是嫁給了那個犯人。

_____

(33) take a/ another dive 急速下墜;快速下掉;直直落(24段)

Otherwise, our stock would have taken another dive.

否則股票又要大跌了。

解析

dive 無論作名詞或動詞解，都表示「由高往低直線下落」。難怪在水裡，指的是「往下潛水」、「向下跳水」，在空中則指的是「向下俯衝」。至於動詞使用 take 以構成 take a dive 則和 take a walk, take a ride 或 take a trip 這些片語裡的用法殊無二致。

小試身手

33. 金價先是緩步爬升，接著急遽下跌。

_____

（34）speak highly of... 誇獎；讚美；表揚（25段）

...he no longer yelled at people, and he tried to speak highly of others.
……但（他）已不再罵人，而且也會盡量說人家的好話。

解析

說人家的好話，把人家捧得高高的 (highly)，對方心裡著實受用。所以 speak highly of... 當然就是「說人家的好話了」，和平常更常見的 speak well of... 大致相同。那說壞話，批評中傷他人呢？把 well 改成 ill，讓片語成為 speak ill of... 就可以了。

還有一個值得學習的地方是 yell at 這個片語，意思是對人「大聲喝斥」。You wouldn't like to be yelled at for no reason, would you?

小試身手

34. 要在人前說他人的好話，別在背後說他們的壞話。

_____

（35）an empty threat 不是真的威脅恫嚇（28段）

What he'd said that afternoon was just an empty threat.
當時他只是亂講的。

解析

這句英譯短短的，可是裡頭大有文章。首先，從句構來說，整個句子的結構是：主詞＋動詞＋主詞補語。現在請對照原文：

What he'd said that afternoon ＋ was ＋ just an empty threat.

你會發現除了主詞，其他都很單純易懂。主詞比較複雜，因為它是個名詞子句（What he'd said that afternoon），何以認定它是名詞子句呢？因為它的後面是動詞，一般說來，動詞之前不外乎就是主詞了，具名詞性質的東西才夠格當主詞，所以這個子句的性質就是名詞子句。

「他是間諜這根本不是個秘密。」怎麼說呢？請把 He's a spy. 這個句子改為名詞子句，再加上 is no secret at all.（Answer: That he's a spy is no secret at all.）

名詞 threat 為「威脅」，有時候是玩真的，要小心以對，因為它是（a real threat）；有時候是裝模作樣，虛張聲勢，不用太過擔心。形容詞 empty 表示「空洞不實」，所以 an empty threat 是哪門子的威脅也就很清楚了。

小試身手

35. 你不可能看得出來他的威脅是真是假。

_____

（36）out of the blue 完全在意料之外；想都沒想到（29段）

Time continued to pass until one day, out of the blue, a very excited Old Chen told me he had something he wanted to show me.

又過了一陣子，老陳忽然興奮得不得了，說有東西要給我看。

解析

out of the blue 這個片語常翻譯為「晴天霹靂」，其實它的本意是「突然而意想不到」，相當於我們平常説的「冷不及防」。你認為「晴天霹靂」和「冷不及防」語意相同嗎？前者比較傾向於指不好、不幸、災難之類的事情突然而至，而後者常指事情（未必是不好、不幸、災難的事情）在沒有心理準備的情況下產生了。

小試身手

36. 老闆事出突然地決定要關掉工廠。

_____

（37）in its entirety 完完整整；原原本本（29段）

It read, in its entirety, as follows:

（信的）全文如下：

解析

讀者先要確認動詞 read 在此為過去式，唸法如 red（紅色）的發音，更重要是它的意義，是「文字內容為……」之意。比如你看到一個牌子，上面寫著「（請）勿（擅）入」，你就可以跟你旁邊的大近視説：The sign reads NO ENTRY.

entire 為形容詞，意思是「全體的、全部的」，它的名詞為 entirety，所以 in its entirety 意思就是「全部」、「完整」，此處指的是一封信，那自然就是「全文」的意思。

as follows 這個習慣語，它的意思倒是簡單，就相當於中文的「如下（所述）」，是個固定用法，就是這兩個字。

小試身手

37-1. 那篇報告整個長達二十頁。

_____

37-2. 以下是我辭職的原因：

_____

（38）take this opportunity to V 利用這個機會來……（31段）

I want to take this opportunity to thank you for changing my life.
我要在這裡謝謝你，因為你改變了我的一生。

解析

成功的人往往是把握機會的人，機會不常有，能看得到機會往往眼光獨到，但是還要進一步「把握機會」take the opportunity，甚至「善用、利用機會」take advantage of/ make good use of the opportunity 才能真正成功。

小試身手

38. 他成功，因為他知道機會在哪裡和如何善用機會。

_____

（39）natural selection（物競）天擇（32段）
　　survival of the fittest 適者生存

I thoroughly believed in natural selection and the survival of the fittest.
我的確相信優勝劣敗，物競天擇的道理。

解析

「物競天擇，適者生存」是達爾文劃時代的進化論的演化原則和結論。不管你信不信，都已被奉為鐵則。從這個殘酷的角度看，社會上每個人都被認為是求生存的競爭者，強者和適者才能在資源有限的環境裡生存，甚至主宰和支配環境裡的資源。其實，對弱勢者，我們是不是該有一份民吾同胞的人文關懷呢？所以有時候不妨在心裡罵上一句：To hell with the abused and misused theory of natural selection and survival of the fittest.

小試身手

39. 他不同情失業的人，因為他相信物競天擇的理論。

_____

（40）（be）in a car accident 出車禍（33段）
　　be weeded out 被剷除；被淘汰

For instance, if I were in a car accident and suffered a concussion that ruined my memory and analytical ability, wouldn't I be "weeded out"?
比方說，萬一我出了車禍，得了腦震盪，記憶力和判斷力都衰退了，我豈不應該被淘汰出局？

解析

首先提醒讀者，這句話裡有個「與現在事實相反的假設」，(if I were..., wouldn't I be...)。

接著來看看「出車禍」，很平常的話吧，可是一時恐怕也不太容易用英文表達，尤其是「出」一字，可能就把讀者的思路帶進死胡同。原來，是 in a car accident 四個簡簡單單的英文字，就把意思帶出來了。當然把 car accident 改為 car crash，成為 in a car crash 也可以。

weed 原本指「野草」、「雜草」，是愛好園藝者的眼中釘，必欲除之（weed out）而後快（註：此處 weed 為動詞），所以 weed out 具有「拔除」、「淘汰」的意思。

小試身手

40. 他出了車禍，但別擔心，他打電話說他只受了點輕傷。

_____

---

(41) a person of mediocre talents 泛泛之輩；平庸之徒（34段）

In the nightmares, I would become a person of very mediocre talents.
夢裡我變成了一個能力十分平庸的人。

解析

句型：「一個……的人」，我們在重點（13）說過了，這裡再多做幾個練習：

a person（man, woman）of...。

「有能力的人」是 a person of ability。

「有才華的人」是 a person of talent。

「有智慧的人」是 a person of wisdom。

如果要強調才華出眾，可以在這些字眼的前面加 great, remarkable 或 incredible 之類的字眼。如果要反其道而行，要說明某位人士平泛無奇，可以在這些名詞之前加個 poor，或如這句英譯加個 mediocre。

41. 她是這麼有音樂天賦的學生，在八歲就開始創作交響樂。

_____

(42) break out in a cold sweat 出一身冷汗（36段）

I was so anxious that I broke out in a cold sweat.
（我）急得一身冷汗。

解析

這個 break out 的用法令人拍案叫絕！請用些氣力，把這麼傳神的片語記下來吧！「急得一身冷汗。」的「急」字就是 anxious，如果你想使用 desperate 或 frantic 來表達也可。

42. 看到他臉上殺氣騰騰的表情，我嚇出一身冷汗來。

_____

(43) live in fearful apprehension 生活在恐懼之中（38段）

Since each Friday night was torture to me, I started dreading Fridays. All through the week I lived in fearful apprehension.
由於每個週五晚上都要被折磨一個晚上，我開始怕週五。整個星期，我真的生活在恐懼之中。

解析

名詞 apprehension 是「心憂」，形容詞 fearful 是「害怕」，因此片語 live in fearful apprehension 自然就是「生活在危疑恐懼之中」。其實無論是名詞

apprehension 或是形容詞 fearful，兩者表示的概念是很接近的，所以如果你要說：live in constant fear 或者 live in constant apprehension 都算正確，都有可能。

小試身手

43. 做過虧心事的人常常活得內心不安。

_____

（44）succumb to（the sleeping pills）受（如安眠藥等之作用或影響而）屈服（39段）

But just as my body was succumbing to the sleeping pills, somehow my mind felt very awake, and I desperately wanted to go on living.

可是安眠藥使我昏沉下去的時候，不知何故，我腦子卻極為清醒，我極想活下去。

解析

succumb to... 這個片語表示一種「因抗拒不了而臣服或屈服」的情況，給人的感覺是毫無招架之力，完全繳械投降。pill(s) 指的是「藥丸」，所以安眠藥就叫作 sleeping pills。

小試身手

44-1. 儘管擔心，她漸漸地讓睡眠征服她。

_____

44-2. 他丟兩顆藥到嘴巴裡，一口把它們吞下。

_____

（45）what does it matter 有何關係（39段）

Then a flash of inspiration came to me: what did it matter if I had no remarkable talents?

我忽然想通了，能力不好又有什麼關係？

解析

這裡有幾個值得一學的地方。首先請看 a flash of inspiration 這個片語，inspiration 是「靈感」，而 flash 是「閃光」，因此 a flash of inspiration 就相當中文「靈光一閃」、「靈光乍現」。

what does it matter，要特別注意 matter 這個字，別看走眼，它是動詞，作「具有重要性的」、「關係重大的」解釋，但是它常用在否定句裡（do, does, did）not matter，以表示「不重要」、「沒關係」。在此則是疑問句，表示「有什麼重要（性）呢？」、「有什麼關係呢？」

小試身手

45. 他要我放心，幾個小錯誤不打緊。他說：「可以不用管它們。」

_____

（46）on the verge of（death）在瀕臨（死亡）之際（39段）

As I sat there on the verge of death, I really wanted to tell him how much I envied him for always being so happy.

在我快死之前，我很想大聲地告訴他，我羨慕你，因為你老是快快樂樂地。

解析

on the verge of（death），介詞 on 表示「接近、快到了」；名詞（the）verge 的本意是某物延伸到最外側的「邊緣」，所以讀者們不妨想想，這個片語是

否因而具備了「快到……的邊緣」，也就是「瀕臨……」。比如：

◈ 那個物種瀕臨絕種。
The species is on the verge of extinction.

◈ 那家公司瀕臨破產（邊緣）。
The company is on the verge of bankruptcy.

小試身手

46. 他幾近(快要)精神失常。

_____

（47）have someone to thank 該感謝（某人）（42段）

I have you to thank for all of this.
這一切都該謝謝你。

解析
也可以用國中就學過的那句：I have to thank you for all of this.「這一切」可以說 all of this，亦可以說 all this。

小試身手

47. 我有今天的成就，要感謝在座的每個人。

_____

（48）文法要點：it is... that...（42段）

...it was because I tried to do such a stupid thing that I finally realized I'm nothing but an ordinary man.

……也虧得我做了這件傻事，我才發現我根本就是個普通的人。

解析

it is... that... 是個句型，也是個重要的文法要點，一般文法書管它叫加強語氣構句，在本書前一、二輯都出現過，非常重要。

句型很簡單是不是？不過就是 it is 和 that。現在請把這個句型去掉，看看結果：

Because I tried to do such a stupid thing, I finally realized I'm nothing but an ordinary man.

如果我們要強調「正是這個原因（because... ）」，就可以把這個原因（because... ）安裝到 it is... that 這個句型的當中去，因為這個句型就相當於中文「正是……」，最後的結果如下：

It was（because I tried to do such a stupid thing）that I finally realized I'm nothing but an ordinary man.

你或許發現上句裡是 It was... 而非 It is...，這是因為這個被強調的部分原本就是過去式（because I tried to do such a stupid thing）。

請看以下兩句中文，哪句語氣強，哪句語氣弱？也就是說，你認為哪一句呼應了這個 it is... that... 的結構呢？

（一）正是因為我做了這件傻事，我才發現我根本就是個普通的人。

（二）因為我做了這件傻事，我才發現我根本就是個普通的人。

小試身手

48. 是他所居之處、而非和他來往之人給他靈感寫出了這部文學鉅著。

_____

(49) cannot help laughing in spite of oneself 忍俊不禁；笑到不行(43段)

The two of us couldn't help laughing in spite of ourselves.
我們兩個人都啞然失笑。

解析

cannot help Ving 是個特殊的用法（cannot help 後面需接動名詞 Ving），具有特殊的含意（忍不住要……；不禁要……）。in spite of 一般作「雖然、儘管」解，但是此處 in spite of oneself 則是傾向「怎麼也克制不了（自己）」的意思。因此 cannot help laughing in spite of oneself 整個就是「實在是無法克制，不由得就笑出來了」。

小試身手

49. 我知道這樣不應該，可是我不由自主地把秘密告訴了她。

_____

(50) as familiar as the taste of home cooking 家常便飯(43段)

To us, the sensation of not being able to vault over a horse in gym or doing poorly on a test was as familiar as the taste of home cooking.
(對我們來說)不會跳木馬，考試考不好，家常便飯也。

解析

大餐固然令人食指大動，家常便飯（home cooking）也是親切（familiar）可口。所以 as familiar as the taste of home cooking 的基本意思即是「如家常便飯（之親切可口），甘之如飴」。

上體育課有跳木馬的經驗嗎？嗯，「跳木馬」的英文終於看到了，有機會學

了，就是 vault over the horse。請注意「跳」字特別用 vault 這個動詞，強調「騰空跳過」，撐竿跳就叫作 pole-vault。

小試身手

50. 這兒沒有什麼奇怪的事。我所見所聞熟悉得和家常便飯一樣。

_____

(51) regret having Vpp 後悔(做了某事)(44)

No doubt he regretted having saved his boss's life.
他一定後悔當年救了總經理一命。

解析

這裡有兩處學習重點，一個為 regret 的用法。有「心懷歉意」和「內心悔恨」兩種不一樣的解釋，而用法也隨之不同。作「心懷歉意」解釋時，後面常需接不定詞 (to V)，比如你想說：

◇ 很抱歉要告訴你，你不能再使用這個辦公室了。
I regret to have to tell you that you may not use this office anymore.

若作「內心悔恨」解釋時，則後面常需要接動名詞 (Ving)，本句即是這樣的用法，而且還更進一步用了完成式形態的動名詞 (having Vpp)，更加把過去做過的動作的意味表達出來。

另一個重點需要注意的是片語 no doubt，本意是「無疑地」，譯者用它來詮釋原著的「一定……」。

小試身手

51. 我很後悔小時候跟媽媽頂嘴。

_____

小試身手解答

1. He is a man of principle and people admire him for it.

2. No matter what people say about him, he just smiles and ignores it.

3. If population growth is not kept under control, it might not only damage a country's economic development but cause other serious social problems as well.

4. He was originally a mechanical engineering major, but he transferred to the electrical engineering department after his freshman year.

5. I had intended to ask her for help, but she had her hands full.

6. It is a well-known story that the business tycoon started out as a rice deliveryman.

7. The box is chock full of odds and ends.

8. He has absolutely no reservations about making his dissatisfaction known to the public.

9. It is self-evident that he's trying to crack a rock with an egg.

10-1. Anyone who wants to meet her in person is required to make an appointment in advance.

10-2. More toilets should be installed exclusively for the handicapped.

11. Usually I take the initiative and strike up a conversation with the passenger sitting next to me.

12. Although the celebrity excelled professionally, he still had a lot of family problems.

13. Nothing can frustrate a man of strong determination.

    有原則的人：a man/ person of principle

    有學問的人（飽學之士）：a man/ person of learning

    有德之人：a man/ person of morality

    有財之人（富人）：a man/ person of wealth　或　a man/ person of means

14. After taking two weeks of sick leave, I don't know how I'll make up for the classes I missed. It will be difficult for me to catch up with my classmates academically.

15. Jim jumped for joy upon hearing the news.

16. I know I am not as smart as my classmates, so I have to work hard to keep from falling behind them.

17. The loss of another ship was a heavy blow to him and his business.

18-1. I pleaded for mercy, but he denied me.

18-2. He sat down and switched on the TV with the remote (control) without saying a word.

19. Not a trace of repentance could be seen on his face.

20. The students thought their teacher was just blowing smoke. What they didn't know was that he'd really lost his temper this time.

21. As word got out, his public image was damaged considerably.

22. Things dragged on like this, neither better nor worse, until no one mentioned it anymore.

23. He has visited the South Pole, not to mention the Great Wall.

24. We're all happy he's back to his old self again.

25. Her letter reads to the effect that she can't make it to the appointment.

26. The vast majority of those present were in favor of building another medical center.

27. In their eyes, perseverance is the most vital factor in learning a new language successfully.

28. We all have a distaste for his exaggerated manner of speaking.

29. This toll-free hotline exists to prevent people from committing suicide.

30. For the time being, I have no intention of emigrating.

31. 第一句：whose 第二句：who

    He was seen entering the building in the company of two of his aides/ assistants.

32. Much to my distress, my sister married the criminal anyway.

33. The price of gold climbed slowly at first, and then took a sudden dive.

34. Speak highly of others in their presence, and don't speak ill of them behind their backs.

35. You can't possibly tell whether his threat is an empty one or a real one.

36. The owner's decision to close down the factory came out of the blue.

37-1. The report, in its entirety, is twenty pages long.

37-2. The reasons for my resignation are as follows:

38. He achieves success because he knows where his opportunities lie and how to take advantage of them.

39. He has no sympathy for the unemployed because he believes in natural selection.

40. He was in a car accident, but don't worry, he called to say he was only slightly hurt.

41. She was a student of such musical talent that she began to compose symphony at eight.

42. I broke out in a cold sweat when I saw the murderous look on his face.

43. People with guilty consciences often live in constant fear.

44-1. Despite her worry, she gradually succumbed to sleep.

44-2. He popped two pills into his mouth and swallowed them in one gulp.

45. He assured me that a few minor mistakes didn't matter. "They're negligible," he said.

46. He is on the verge of losing his mind.

47. I have everyone sitting now here in this room to thank for what I am today.

48. It was where he lived rather than whom he associated with that inspired him to produce such a literary masterpiece.

49. I knew I shouldn't, but I told her the secret in spite of myself.

50. Nothing feels strange to me here. Everything I hear and see is as familiar as the taste of home cooking.

51. I regret having talked back to my mom when I was a kid.

The Stories of Three Children
三個孩子的故事

1-5　　不講話的孩子

　　第一次看到這個孩子的時候，是三十四年前了，當時我在大學念書，推著腳踏車正要上學，看到一位警察用繩子牽著一個小孩子在街上走，孩子大概不到十歲，沒有穿上衣，又瘦又黑，雙手被綁在身後，另外一條繩子將他五花大綁，繩子一端由警察拉住，將他像牽狗一樣地在街上牽著走，我還注意到他沒有穿鞋子。三十年前，汽車很少，警車也少，警察抓了犯人，常常只好在路上將犯人拉拉扯扯地帶去警局。這個孩子顯然犯了法，被警伯逮到，正在押送到警局去。

　　因為犯人太小，路人忍不住要問，這是怎麼一回事？這位警察索性停了下來，向大家解釋。原來這孩子的媽媽去世，爸爸生了病，躺在床上，孩子一再出去偷東西養家，雖然只是偷點吃的東西，可是被偷的店家忍無可忍；今天早上將他抓到以後，就不再放他。

　　我注意到這孩子的表情，別人在這種情況下，應該只會有兩種表

◇ drag（v.）拖　　　　　　　　　　◇ loop（v.）纏繞
◇ skinny（adj.）瘦巴巴的　　　　　◇ criminal（n.）罪犯
◇ swarthy（adj.）（指膚色）黝黑的　◇ evidently（adv.）顯然地

The child who never spoke

The first time I saw this child was thirty-four years ago, back when I was in college. As I was pushing my bike on my way to class, I saw a policeman dragging a boy down the street with a rope. Shirtless, skinny and swarthy, he probably wasn't yet ten years old. His hands were bound behind his back, and another rope looped through his legs and around his neck held them in place. Holding one end of the rope, the policeman pulled him along the street like a dog. I also noticed that he wore no shoes. Thirty years ago, there weren't many cars, including police cars, so when policemen caught criminals, they often had to get them to the station by dragging them through the streets. Evidently, the boy had broken the law, been caught by the officer and was being taken to the police station.

Because this lawbreaker was so small, passersby couldn't resist asking what in the world it was that he had done, so the officer decided he might as well stop and explain the situation to everyone. The boy's mother was dead and his dad was bedridden with illness, so he repeatedly went out and stole things to take care of his family. Even though he only stole a little food each time, the shop owners he took it from had endured all they could put up with. When they caught him again this morning, they didn't let him go.

I noticed the expression on the boy's face. Had anyone else been in his place, he would most likely have had one of two expressions:

◇ lawbreaker (n.) 違／犯法者
◇ passerby (n.) 路人 (複數為passersby)
◇ bedridden (adj.) 無法起身離床的

◇ repeatedly (adv.) 重複地
◇ endure (v.) 忍受
◇ expression (n.) 表情

情：一種是滿不在乎的叛逆表情，不然就是羞愧地抬不起頭來。而這孩子呢？我們可以說他是副茫然的表情，或者可以說是毫無表情，對我們這些路人，他一點也不逃避我們的目光，只是不斷地掙扎，顯然他被綁得太緊了。

　　我當時是監獄裡的義工，因此我不久就在看守所裡遇到了這孩子，他仍沒有上衣，赤著腳，在掃地。我找了一位熱心的管理員，提醒他這孩子似乎沒有上衣可穿，他立即去找了一件紅色的小孩襯衫給他穿上。他說這孩子安靜極了，從不講話。根據他的觀察，他被關到看守所之後，似乎沒有說任何一句話，可是非常服從，叫他做事，他也會乖乖的做，從不埋怨。他也說這孩子沒有什麼表情。這是我第二次看到這孩子。

　　第三次看到這孩子，是個大雨天，外面下大雨，裡面來了大批蒼蠅，正好有什麼大官來訪，這位孩子被管理員抓來在走廊裡拍地上的蒼蠅，可是他技術不太好，並沒有打到很多的蒼蠅。

◇ rebelliousness (n.) 叛逆　　　　　◇ volunteer (n.) 志工；義工
◇ vacant (adj.) 空的　　　　　　　◇ encounter (v.) 遇見；碰到
◇ bystander (n.) 旁人　　　　　　　◇ barefooted (adj.) 打赤腳的
◇ struggle (v.) 掙扎　　　　　　　◇ warmhearted (adj.) 熱心的；好心的

either devil-may-care rebelliousness or head-hanging shame. But this boy? You could say his expression was vacant, or that he had no expression at all. He made no effort whatsoever to escape the stares of us bystanders. He only struggled continually—it was clear that he had been tied up too tightly.

At that time I was a volunteer at the jail, so it wasn't long before I encountered the child at the guardhouse there. Still shirtless and barefooted, he was sweeping the floor. I found a warmhearted guard and brought his attention to the fact that the boy seemed to have no shirt to wear. Immediately he went and got a red children's shirt for him. He said that he was a very taciturn child—as far as he knew, he hadn't said a word since being locked up in the guardhouse. He was extremely obedient, though—if you told him to do something, he'd go right off and do it without complaining. He also said that the boy's face seemed expressionless. This was my second encounter with the boy.

The third time I saw him was on a very rainy day. As the rain poured down outside, a swarm of flies had come in. It just so happened that some important official was visiting that day, so the boy had been assigned by the guard to swat the flies on the ground in the hallway. He wasn't very good at it, though—he hadn't managed to swat very many of them.

◇ taciturn (adj.) 寡言的；話少的　　◇ swarm (n.) 群 (尤其指昆蟲)
◇ obedient [əˋbidɪənt] (adj.) 聽話的；乖巧的　　◇ assign (v.) 指派 (定)
◇ expressionless (adj.) 面無表情的　　◇ swat (v.) (用力) 拍；打

6-10　　我反正沒有什麼事做，就拿過他的蒼蠅拍，替他打。在我打了一陣以後，這個孩子忽然抱住了我，將他的頭伏在我的肩上，他仍然不說一句話，可是我感到他的淚水滴在我的肩膀上。

　　我蹲在那裡，不知如何是好，這個不說話的孩子，終於用他的肢體語言向大家述說他的心情，一個十歲的小孩子，被人五花大綁地遊街示眾，可以想像得到他心中有多少的悲苦。恐怕他這一輩子，只被人打罵，只被人追趕，從來沒有人關心過他。流在我肩上的淚水，顯然是感激的淚水。

　　有人來將他拉走，整個走廊裡鴉雀無聲。在看守所，我相信這種安靜是特別的情形。我趁大官來以前，趕快走了。

　　有好一陣子，我在學校裡變得沉默寡言。同學們都不知道我為什麼變成了一位不說話的大孩子，同學們談出國計畫、談交女朋友、談舞會。我卻老是在想那位生病的老先生和他那位不和別人說話的兒子。

◇ flyswatter (n.) 蒼蠅拍
◇ squat [skwɑt] (v.) 蹲
◇ body language (n.) 肢體語言
◇ parade [pəˋred] (v.) 遊街；遊行
◇ chase (v.) 追逐；追趕
◇ affection (n.) 感情；關懷

6-10

Since I had nothing better to do, I took his flyswatter and swatted flies for him. After I had been swatting for a while, the boy suddenly threw his arms around me and buried his head in my shoulder. He still didn't say a word, but I could feel his tears dripping onto my shoulder.

I squatted there, not knowing what to do. This silent child had finally expressed his feelings through body language. You can imagine what bitterness and pain a ten-year-old boy who had been hog-tied and paraded through the streets in front of everyone must have felt. It was likely that for his whole life, he had only been beaten, yelled at and chased away; no one had ever showed affection for him before. The tears he was shedding on my shoulder were clearly tears of gratitude.

Someone came and pulled him away; afterward, the entire corridor was still. I bet that kind of quiet was a rarity in the guardhouse. I hurried and left before the important official arrived.

For a fairly long time after that, I became quiet and reserved at school. None of my classmates understood why I had become a big kid who wouldn't talk. They talked about their plans to travel abroad, talked about their love lives, talked about dances. But I kept thinking about that sick old man and his son who never spoke to anyone.

◇ gratitude (n.) 感激
◇ corridor (n.) 走道；走廊

◇ rarity (n.) 罕見之物；罕有之事
◇ reserved (adj.) 緘默的；有所保留的

不肯吃飯的孩子

　　這個孩子傻傻的，孤兒院的修女告訴我他有點智能不足，不是很嚴重，他可以照顧自己。可是不會念書，在學校裡念的是啟智班。

11-15　　我每次問他任何問題，他都回答「不知道」，真把我氣得半死。

　　他腿部受傷了，修女把他送進了醫院，他的祖父是他的唯一親人，趕到醫院來陪他，因為修女不能二十四小時陪他。

　　他忽然不吃東西，因為是外傷，沒有什麼理由不吃東西，怎麼樣哄他，每次他都只吃一兩口青菜，其他什麼都不碰，他的祖父看他不吃，就將他的食物吃得一乾二淨，兩天下來，他仍只吃些青菜，祖父急了，趕緊打電話將修女找來。

　　這位對他頗為了解的修女也百思不得其解，她知道這孩子向來胃口

◇ orphanage (n.) 孤兒院
◇ mentally (adv.) 心智上；智能上
◇ handicapped (adj.) 殘障的
◇ severely [səˋvɪrlɪ] (adv.) 嚴重地

◇ frustrate (v.) 使 (某人) 沮喪
◇ relative (n.) 親人
◇ inexplicably [ɪnˋɛksplɪkəblɪ] (adv.) 無法解釋地

The child who wouldn't eat

This child was rather slow—the nun at the orphanage told me he was somewhat mentally handicapped, but not so severely that he couldn't take care of himself. He couldn't read, though, and he was in the special needs class at school.

Every time I asked him a question, he would always answer, "I don't know." It frustrated me half to death.

He hurt his leg, and a nun took him to the hospital. His grandfather, his only relative, hurried over to the hospital to be with him because the nuns couldn't be by his side twenty-four hours a day.

Then, inexplicably, he stopped eating. Because his injury was external, there was no reason for him not to eat, but no matter how we coaxed him at mealtimes, he would only eat a couple mouthfuls of green vegetables and leave the rest of his food untouched. When he saw that his grandson wouldn't eat, the boy's grandfather would finish off the remainder of the food himself. For two days straight, the boy ate nothing but vegetables. Finally his grandfather got worried and called in a nun to help.

The nun, who understood the boy quite well, was at a loss to explain why he wouldn't eat. He had always had a prodigious

◇ external (adj.) 外部的
◇ remainder (n.) 剩餘；殘留
◇ straight (adv.) 連續；接連
◇ prodigious [prə'dɪdʒəs] (adj.) 驚人的；異於常人的

奇佳，不吃東西必定有原因。可是究竟是什麼原因呢？

　　還是這位修女厲害，她猜這位孩子一定是怕他的祖父太窮，買不起東西吃，只好自己不吃，讓他的祖父吃個痛快。他祖父果真吃了，這下他更加相信只有自己挨餓才能使祖父有東西吃。

16-20　　修女去樓下買了兩個便當，一個給他的祖父，一個自己吃。他們一開始吃，這孩子立刻餓虎撲羊地將醫院送來的飯菜搶來大吃特吃，不僅吃完了醫院的伙食，還要修女去買一盒便當給他吃。

　　孩子同病房的病友們都鬆了一口氣，醫生護士都來看他吃飯，房裡幾乎要開一個慶祝會。

只能祈禱的孩子

　　第一次在兒童中心看到這個孩子，大概是四年前，孩子只有六歲左右，跳跳蹦蹦地。他自動告訴我，「我媽媽走得太早，爸爸要做工，

◇ appetite（n.）胃口；食慾
◇ eventually（adv.）最後
◇ ensure（v.）保證；擔保

◇ convince（v.）令（某人）相信
◇ boxed lunch（n.）便當
◇ pounce（v.）猛撲

appetite—there must be some reason why he wouldn't eat now. But what could it be?

Eventually the nun figured it out. She guessed that the boy was afraid his grandfather was too poor to buy food for himself, so in his mind, not eating his food was the only way he could ensure that his grandfather would enjoy a good, square meal. Just as he'd expected, his grandfather ate the food, which further convinced him that he could only feed his grandfather by going hungry.

The nun went downstairs and bought two boxed lunches: one for the boy's grandfather and one for herself. The moment they began to eat, the boy tore into his hospital food like a tiger pouncing on its prey. Not only did he make short work of his hospital food, he also asked the nun to buy another boxed lunch for him.

16-20

The patients who were in the same room as the boy breathed a collective sigh of relief. All the doctors and nurses came to see him eat; there was practically a celebration in the room.

The child who could only pray

It was about four years ago when I saw this child for the first time in a children's care center. He was only about six years old then, but he was bursting with energy. "My mom left us too early," he told me of his own volition, "and my dad can't take care of me because he has

◇ prey (n.) 獵物　　　　　　　　◇ bursting (adj.) 旺盛的；飽滿的
◇ collective (adj.) 集體的

無法照顧我，只好送我到這裡來」，我當時聽了很難過，因為這位只有六歲的孩子居然用「我媽媽走得太早」這種詞句。

　　四年來，孩子越來越高。大約在聖誕節前幾天，我走進這所兒童中心的教堂，又看到了這個孩子，當時教堂裡空無一人，只有這個孩子跪在聖母像前祈禱。

　　我問他是怎麼一回事，他說：「我爸爸生病了，我是一個小孩，沒有能力替爸爸請好的醫生，只好祈求聖母保佑爸爸。」

21-25　　在我離開教堂的時候，忍不住再回頭看一下，教堂裡聖母像前面有一些燃燒的蠟燭，孩子跪在聖母面前，抬著頭，燭光照在他的臉上，遠遠看去，極像一幅美麗的圖畫，也極適合用在聖誕卡上。

　　我當時就替孩子的爸爸高興，有幾個人能有如此孝順的孩子？

後記

　　第一個孩子很快就出獄了，他的爸爸，在一些善心的監獄管理人員湊足醫藥費以後，總算恢復了健康，以當時的經濟情況，這些薪水微

◇ sadden (v.) 使 (某人) 傷心難過
◇ deserted (adj.) 荒廢的；無人的
◇ Virgin Mary (n.) 聖母
◇ portrait (n.) 畫像；肖像

to work, so he brought me here." It saddened me to hear the words "My mom left us too early" coming from the mouth of a mere six-year-old.

For four years, the boy grew taller and taller. I walked into the chapel of the children's center a few days before Christmas and saw him again. At the time, the chapel was deserted; only the boy was there, kneeling in front of the Virgin Mary, praying.

I asked him what had happened. "My dad is sick," he said. "I'm just a kid, so I have no way of getting a good doctor to come and see him. All I can do is pray for Mary to watch over him."

As I left the chapel, I couldn't resist looking back over my shoulder. There were candles burning in front of the portrait of the Virgin Mary. The boy was kneeling there, his head raised, the candlelight illuminating his face. From a distance, it looked like a beautiful picture, perfect for the front of a Christmas card.

21-25

I felt happy for the child's father. How many people have such filial children?

Epilogue

The first child was soon released from jail. After some kindhearted prison guards collected enough money to buy medicine for him,

◇ illuminate (v.) 照亮
◇ filial (adj.) 恭敬的；孝順的
◇ release (v.) 釋放

薄的管理人員一定必須節衣縮食好幾個月，才湊足這筆錢。

　　幾位台大電機系的學生在這孩子出獄以後，志願替他補習功課，他也開始和他們說話。

　　關於第二個孩子，由於他在醫院裡老是不講話，醫院的一批專家終於給了他一紙證明，說他有某種程度的智障，使他拿到了一份殘障手冊，將來可以享受一些政府給殘障者的福利。智障的孩子如此的孝順，大家都沒有想到。

26-27　關於第三個孩子，他爸爸的病不嚴重，孩子知道他爸爸病好了以後，心情好了很多，我看到他的時候，又在跳跳蹦蹦了。

　　我從未在孩提時代受過什麼苦，可是我卻有機會碰到很多窮苦的孩子，他們顯然渴望我們的關懷，任何我們給予他們的愛心，都像灑在乾旱田地上的雨水，絕對是他們渴望的，可是更重要的是，這些窮苦孩子似乎比其他的孩子更有愛心、更有孝心。

◇ recover (v.) 恢復
◇ economy [ɪˋkɑnəmɪ] (n.) 經濟
◇ scrimp (v.) 省吃儉用；節約
◇ virtually (adv.) 幾乎；幾近
◇ certificate (n.) 證明
◇ disabled (adj.) 殘障的；失能的

his father finally recovered his health. Considering the state of the economy at the time, those poorly paid guards must have had to scrimp and save for months to collect such a sum.

A few electronics students from NTU volunteered to help the boy with his homework after he got out of jail. After a while, he started talking to them.

As for the second child, because he virtually never spoke while in the hospital, some experts there finally gave him a certificate that said he was mentally handicapped to a certain degree. They also got him a handbook for the disabled so that in the future he could receive disability benefits from the government. Everyone was amazed that a mentally handicapped boy could be so filial.

As for the third child, his father's illness wasn't too severe. After he learned his dad had recovered, he cheered up quite a bit. When I saw him after that, he was bouncing off the walls again.

26-27

I never suffered much in my childhood, but I've had opportunities to meet many less fortunate children who clearly want to be loved by people like us. Any love that we give them is like rain falling on a parched field—just what they have been thirsting for. But more importantly, these poor children actually seem to be more loving and filial than other children.

◇ disability benefits (n.) 殘障福利
◇ bounce (v.) 彈跳
◇ parched (adj.) (因乾旱或缺水而) 裂的

◇ thirst (v.) 口渴 (常引申為「渴求」；「想望」)

（1）hold... in place 把……定住（使不能動彈）（1段）

His hands were bound behind his back, and another rope looped through his legs and around his neck held them in place.

（他的）雙手被綁在身後，另外一條繩子將他五花大綁。

解析

把某東西的位置固定好，不使之隨意移動換位，英文就以 hold... in place 這個片語來表達。就像骨折時，醫師會先把骨折的部分接好、固定好，打上石膏，利用人體的癒合能力，讓斷骨能夠接合痊癒。打石膏的作用不外乎就是讓剛接好的部分不至於移位。這麼說來，東西的位置錯置了，是否可以用 (something) go out of place 來表達呢？你身邊有字典嗎？可以翻開它來求證。

小試身手

1. 他把引擎蓋放回原來位置，回到車上，這次成功地啟動了車子。

　　_____

（2）break the law 犯／違法（1段）

Evidently the boy had broken the law, been caught by the officer and was being taken to the police station.

這個孩子顯然犯了法，被警伯逮到，正在押送到警局去。

解析

法紀法律是社會的綱常，無法可依循，社會會動盪不安。

「立法 (make the law)」的人叫作「立法委員 (lawmaker)」。「執法 (enforce the law)」的官員叫「執法者 (law enforcement officer)」。

一般民眾大多是「守法 (law-abiding)」的人；少數是「犯法 (break the law)」的人。

2. 他招認犯了法，並且說他絕對不會迴避應得的懲罰。

_____

(3) what in the world 到底／究竟什麼事情；(2段)

　　might as well 乾脆⋯⋯；索性⋯⋯；倒不如⋯⋯算了

Because this lawbreaker was so small, passersby couldn't resist asking what in the world it was that he had done, so the officer decided he might as well stop and explain the situation to everyone.

因為犯人太小，路人忍不住要問，這是怎麼一回事？這位警察索性停了下來，向大家解釋。

解析

請讀者們想想看 What are you doing here? 和 What in the world are you doing here? 何差別？第二句比起第一句話應該多了些「不耐煩、不高興」的弦外之音吧！其實幾乎每個疑問詞 (Wh~) 後面接著 in the world 或 on earth 都會有這樣的意味，以下多提供幾個給大家參考。

Who in the world made you do this?
Where on earth did you come by this?
Why in the world didn't he move out of that neighborhood?

另一個要點是 might as well ——這個由助動詞所構成的片語，意思相當於「乾脆⋯⋯」、「索性⋯⋯」。表示某人在一種心不甘情不願的心態下去做某事。比方，夏日炎炎，朋友約你到游泳池戲水消暑或者逛街購物，你心裡盤算一番，覺得「倒不如」在家睡覺吹冷氣，這時你就可以說 I might as well stay home where it's air-conditioned and sleep.

（4）be bedridden with illness 臥病在床；纏綿病榻（2段）

The boy's mother was dead and his dad was bedridden with illness, so he repeatedly went out and stole things to take care of his family.

原來這孩子的媽媽去世，爸爸生了病，躺在床上，孩子一再出去偷東西養家。

解析

看到片語中最核心的字眼 bedridden 開頭的那三個字母 bed 了嗎？那不就是「床（榻）」嗎？所以 be bedridden with illness 和中文的「臥病在床」不剛好就是絕配嗎？語言之妙有時就是妙在這裡，明明是生活在兩個不同地方的人，在看人生百態、萬事景物的時候，說法有時候是那麼的雷同。你能否想出幾個類似的東西來呢？我這裡有兩個：中文有「輕如鴻毛」，英文有 as light as a feather；中文說「賤如糞土」，英文就說 dirt cheap。

(5) put up with 忍受（2段）

Even though he only stole a little food each time, the shop owners he took it from had endured all they could put up with.

雖然只是偷點吃的東西，可是被偷的店家忍無可忍。

解析

簡單幾個字的組合，往往讓人如墜五里霧中── put up with 怎麼會跑出一個「忍受」的意思來？英語為母語的人，可以不太費力地把這個片語學起來，我們可能就得費比母語人士五倍十倍的力氣來學習了。

回到主題來做練習，哪些東西常是我們受不了的呢？「廢話、胡說八道（nonsense）」讓人受不了；「讓人久候（keeping somebody waiting）」也是；還有「倨傲、瞧不起人（arrogance）」也是吧？

◆ 我受不了你的胡扯了。
I can't put up with your nonsense anymore.

◆ 你怎麼受得了人家讓你等這麼久？
How can you put up with being kept waiting for so long?

◆ 沒有幾個人受得了他的勢利。
Few people could put up with his arrogance.

小試身手

5. 沒有人能忍受他的壞脾氣，連他的家人也受不了。

_____

(6) (be)in someone's place 異地而處；處在(某人的)景況(3 段)

Had anyone else been in his place, he would most likely have had one of two expressions...

別人在這種情況下，應該只會有兩種表情……

解析

在這個重點裡，讀者可以學到重要的片語：(be)in someone's place；還有在前兩輯介紹過的文法觀念：倒裝和假設語氣。

(be)in someone's place 意為「處在某人的景況」。這個片語並不難理解，比較困難的是它的用法。因為它本身的意義的關係，一定要用在假設語氣裡。各位想想看，「換成我是你，我就……」，說真的，我再怎麼也不可能成為你，所以這是一種與事實完全相反的假想情況，是必須用假設語氣(的動詞)來表現的。例如：如果你的身分的確是學生，那你可以說：I am a student 或 I go to school 之類的話。可是，如果你目前的身分不是學生，可是你卻嚮往當個學生，這時你可能想說，「倘使我是學生，我就會熱愛所有學科。」—— If I were a student, I would enjoy every subject I studied.

讀者們，注意到(假設法)動詞 were 和 would enjoy 了吧！他們是不是和原來的 am 和 enjoy 不一樣呢？因此，是 were 和 would enjoy 把「與事實相反」的意思表現出來，而不是如一般初學者所容易誤解的 if(如果、倘使)那個字。何以見得？因為我們可以把句子以倒裝的結構，寫成 Were I a student, I would enjoy every subject I studied. 由 If I were a student... 到 Were I a student... 的這種轉變(你看出哪個字被省略了、哪個字被調動了位置嗎？)，就叫作倒裝，如此便可加強語氣。

現在我們回過頭來看看原英譯：

Had anyone else been in his place, he would most likely have had one of two expressions...

很明顯這個句子倒裝了，我們現在把它還原：

If anyone else had been in his place, he would most likely have had one of two expressions...

我們認定它是個使用假設語氣的句子，何以見得呢？證據就在 had... been... 和 would... have had... 這兩個動詞，為什麼和之前洋洋灑灑長篇大論裡的 were 和 would enjoy（If I were a student, I would enjoy every subject I studied.）不一樣呢？因為它們一個是「與現在事實相反」的假設語氣，而一個是「與過去事實相反」的假設。

假設語氣規則如下：

與現在事實相反：...were..., would enjoy...（動詞用過去式）
與過去事實相反：...had been..., would have had...（動詞用過去完成式）

以下練習請讀者依實際狀況去思考要如何表達：

小試身手

6-1. 倘若你是我，你也會這麼做。

_____

6-2. 倘若我生在美國，我的英語就會說得流利了。

_____

(7) no... whatsoever 根本沒有……;連……都沒有(3段)

He made no effort whatsoever to escape the stares of us bystanders.

對我們這些路人,他一點也不逃避我們的目光。

解析

掌握一個原則,就可以把這要點學好,即 whatsoever 這個字裝飾功能多過於實用價值。把 whatsoever 拿掉,句子依然成立,而且對句意影響不大。這就像一位貴婦,少戴顆鑽戒,只是少了點富貴氣,貴婦還是貴婦。

這裡的 no... whatsoever 跟 not... at all 的意思差不多。你想把英譯改成 He made no effort at all to escape the stares of us bystanders. 也可。

若有人愛信口雌黃,隨口亂說,久而久之,沒人相信他的話,這時你可以說:「她現在已經一點信用都沒有。」—— She no longer has any credibility whatsoever.

小試身手

7. 對於窮人,他絲毫沒有慈悲。

_____

(8) bring someone's attention to the fact that... 請某人注意到某個事實(4段)

I found a warmhearted guard and brought his attention to the fact that the boy seemed to have no shirt to wear.

我找了一位熱心的管理員,提醒他這孩子似乎沒有上衣可穿。

解析

這個片語重要,卻不難學。把 pay attention to(注意),當中的 attention 拿到這裡來用,bring someone's attention to the fact 當然就具備了「讓某某

人注意到某個事實」的含意，其後再用一個 that 子句來說明事實為何。

這個片語可以靈活變化，比如「他要我注意到掛在房間角落裡的那幅畫像。」—— He directed my attention to the portrait hanging in the corner of the room. 動詞改為 directed，而此句不必加 "the fact that..."。

小試身手

8. 你需要讓他注意到輿論不利於他的事實。

　　_____

（9）since Ving 自從……（4段）

...as far as he knew, he hadn't said a word since being locked up in the guardhouse.

根據他的觀察，他被關到看守所後，似乎沒有說任何一句話。

解析

since 有多種詞性，常見的是作連接詞和介詞使用，也可以作副詞用。讀者們應該比較習慣作連接詞使用，如：She has been performing well since she started high school. —— since 引導一個（時間）副詞子句，有主詞 she，有動詞 began。

也正因為習於這樣的用法，反而造成有些人對 since 作介詞不甚理解。其實只要改成 since her first day of high school，這個 since 就成了介詞，後接一個名詞片語了。

本文的 since 便是介詞的用法，若要改寫為連接詞的用法，結果會如下：

As far as he knew, he hadn't said a word since he was locked up in the guardhouse.

讀者體會到了吧，因為 he 和 was 的加入，since 搖身一變為連接詞，一個子句於焉成形。

小試身手

9. 自從搬到這裡以來，我們的生活似乎變得更好。

_____

（10）It just so happens that... 剛好……；碰巧……（5段）

It just so happened that some important official was visiting that day...
（當天）正好有什麼大官來訪……

解析

如果你在某場合擔任英文傳譯，我方發言人冒出一句，「無巧不成書，一輛警車剛好巡邏到那一帶。」你就可以使用 It just so happens that... 這個句型來翻譯「無巧不成書……」這句話：

It just so happened that a police car was patrolling in that neighborhood.

小試身手

10. 我們正好有你要找的零件。

_____

(11)It is likely that... 很可能(7段)

It was likely that for his whole life, he had only been beaten, yelled at and chased away; no one had ever showed affection for about him before.

恐怕他這一輩，只被人打罵，只被人追趕，從來沒有人關心過他。

解析

likely 是這個句型的關鍵字眼，對初學者而言，千萬不要因為學過了 like 就以為掌握了 likely。兩個字無論就意義、就用法，根本是兩碼子事。

在句型裡 likely 為形容詞，意義為「可能的」，但是又和一般讀者習見的 possible 不完全相同，likely 的機率要比 possible 來得高，用法也有別。

likely 可以「人」為主詞：

(○)My aunt is likely to visit us next week.

而 possible 就不可以：

(×)My aunt is possible to visit us next week.

科學家說，地球不斷在暖化，以致高山和極地的冰河冰帽不斷地消融。有可能整個融化掉嗎？真令人杞人憂「冰」。不過那是千百年後的事，讀者先煩惱如何因應以下挑戰。特別注意是「不可能」喔。

小試身手

11. 兩極的冰帽不可能會融掉。

_____

（12）the remainder of something 剩下來的……東西（13段）

When he saw that his grandson wouldn't eat, the boy's grandfather would finish off the remainder of the food himself.

他的祖父看他不吃，就將他的食物吃得一乾二淨。

解析

剩下或殘留的部分就是 the remainder，所以「還沒喝完的湯」是 the remainder of the soup；「還沒看完的故事」是 the remainder of the story；「三分之二的士兵駐守那裡，而其餘的被調回。」就要以 Two-thirds of the soldiers were stationed there, while the remainder were sent back. 來表示（本句在較不正式的用法中，也可用 rest 取代 remainder）。

小試身手

12. 我們剩下的假期就逛博物館和購物。

_____

（13）（be）at a loss to V 不知道要怎麼……；無從解釋……（14段）

The nun, who understood the boy quite well, was at a loss to explain why he wouldn't eat.

這位對他頗為了解的修女也百思不得其解。

解析

at a loss 本身為「茫然」、「不知所措」，以下範例讓讀者更進一步熟悉 (be)at a loss... 這個句型：

◇ 我腦海一片空白，不知道怎麼作答試卷上的每個題目。

My brain went blank and I was at a loss to come up with the right answer for each question in the test paper.

然而，at a loss 後面不是接 to V 的時候，句型變成「at a loss + as to + 疑問副詞子句」；或是「at a loss + for + 名詞」：

◈ 她似乎不曉得怎麼掌控狀況。
She seems to be at a loss as to how to get the situation under control.

◈ 我啞口無言。
I was at a loss for words.

小試身手

13. 我根本不曉得該到哪裡去求助 (seek for help)。

_____

---

(14) just as someone expects 如某人所料 (15段)

Just as he'd expected, his grandfather ate the food, which further convinced him that he could only feed his grandfather by going hungry.
他祖父果真吃了，這下他更加相信只有自己挨餓才能使祖父有東西吃。

解析
很實用的句型。「一如某人所料」，無論哪種語言，都會有這種話吧。一件事情發生次數多了，讓人憑經驗就可以預知下次發生的結果。

◈ 果然如我所料，叔叔送我筆記型電腦當作聖誕禮物。
Just as I had expected, my uncle sent me a notebook computer as a Christmas gift.

讀者們，如我所料，你們應該頗能掌握這個句型了，最後提醒各位，不要以為這個句型非用過去完成式（had Vpp）不可，其他的時態也常使用於這個句型裡。比如：

◈ 我很肯定我們的球隊會贏，正如大家所期望。
I have no doubt our team will win, just as everyone expects we will.

小試身手

14. 那個消息果然如我所料，非常地振奮人心（encouraging）。

_____

（15）be bursting with energy 渾身是勁；活力充沛（18段）

He was only about six years old then, but he was bursting with energy.
孩子只有六歲左右，跳跳蹦蹦地。

解析

從英譯來看，看不出來跳或蹦，譯者在這裡採用意譯的方式來處理中文的「跳跳蹦蹦」。burst 的意思是「脹破」、「爆炸」，這裡是比喻的用法，形容孩子的活力塞得滿滿的，到快要爆出來的程度。

小試身手

15. 我以為她跑完了賽跑以後會有些倦意，沒想到她仍然體力充沛。

_____

（16）have no way of Ving 沒有辦法……（20段）

I'm just a kid, so I have no way of getting a good doctor to come and see him.

我是一個小孩，沒有能力替爸爸請好的醫生。

解析

句型 have no way of Ving 表示「沒有辦法……」或「……無能為力」。比如：

◈ 我無從得知他的下落。
I have no way of knowing his whereabouts.

◈ 我沒有辦法說服他離開那棟鬧鬼的屋子。
I have no way of persuading him to move out of the haunted house.

小試身手

16. 上不了網，我沒辦法知道哪家餐廳料理最好的牛肉麵。

_____

（17）cannot resist Ving 忍不住……（21段）

As I left the chapel, I couldn't resist looking back over my shoulder.
在我離開教堂的時候，忍不住再回頭看一下。

解析

這個句型牽涉到 cannot resist 的用法，非常重要！在意義上，它是「忍不住……」的意思，在用法上，它後面接著忍不住想做的動作，和常見的 cannot help Ving 都相當接近。resist 因為本身為「抗拒」的意思，所以 cannot resist Ving 帶有「很想做某事，到壓抑不住的程度」（cannot control the urge to V...）的意味，而 cannot help Ving 傾向表示消極性地「不得不……」、「別無它法只能……」（have no choice but to V...）。

◇ 我忍不住叫一個巧克力冰淇淋甜筒。
I couldn't resist ordering a chocolate ice cream cone.

◇ 我不禁為他感到難過。
I couldn't help feeling sorry for him.

小試身手

17. 我忍不住親親那個嬰兒可愛的臉龐。

_____

（18）considering... 就……考量；從……來看（23段）
　　　scrimp and save 省吃儉用

Considering the state of the economy at the time, those poorly paid guards must have had to scrimp and save for months to collect such a sum.
以當時的經濟狀況，這些薪水微薄的管理人員一定必須節衣縮食好幾個月，才湊足這筆錢。

解析

打開字典查 considering 這個字，當字典告訴你，它是介詞時，你會嚇一大跳吧？當然字典的權威性是不容懷疑的，讀者們，請接受這個事實：considering 是介詞，真的是。如果你使用英文而想表達「就……考量；從……來看」，就請用 considering 這個字。譬如：

◇ 考慮到預算拮据，我們決定捨搭飛機改搭巴士。
Considering our budget constraints, we decided to travel by bus instead of by plane.

另外一個很值得學習的重點為 scrimp and save 這個片語。save 為「儲蓄」、「節省」。而 scrimp 則已到了斤斤計較、錙銖必較、「能省則省」、「能不花就不花」的程度了。兩個同義而不同程度的字放在一起，把「省吃儉用」和「節衣縮食」的精神發揮得淋漓盡致。最後特別提醒讀者，動詞 scrimp 後常接介詞 on，所以「我告訴他，醫療的錢省不得。」英文要表示為：I told him not to scrimp on (money for) personal medical care.

小試身手

18-1. 以他獲得諾貝爾獎的年紀而論，我們應該加倍推崇他。

_____

18-2. 我們家得節衣縮食才買得起 (afford) 新的電腦。〔用未來式〕

_____

（19）thirst for... 渴求……（27段）

Any love that we give them is like rain falling on a parched field—just what they have been thirsting for.

任何我們給予他們的愛心，都像灑在乾旱田地上的雨水，絕對是他們渴望的。

解析

thirst 常作名詞用，可是在英譯裡卻當起動詞（have been thirsting）來了。口渴是生理的反應，口乾舌燥，當然希望喝點東西來解渴。但是人類的「飢渴」，除卻口渴腹饑的生理現象，也往往對精神及性靈層次的東西有一種如飢似渴的欲求，以英文表達，就是 hunger for 或 thirst for，介詞 for 後接著想望渴求的目標。

如果把 hunger 和 thirst 這兩個動詞分別改成形容詞 hungry 和 thirsty，還是表達相同的意思，但是在使用上常得在前面加個 be 動詞，使之成為 be hungry（thirsty）for 的形式。

其實 hunger 和 thirst 更常作名詞使用，在這情況下，可以把片語改為 have a hunger/ thirst for，譬如：

◇ 她求知若渴／饑。
She has an insatiable thirst/ hunger for knowledge.

小試身手

19. 他極希望有機會服務他的國家。

_____

小試身手解答

1. He put the hood back in place, went back into the car and succeeded in starting it this time.

2. He confessed to breaking the law and said he would never seek to avoid the punishment he deserved.

3-1. Who in the world made you believe such a ridiculous explanation?

3-2. Instead of sticking with such a lousy job, I might as well just quit.

4. He has been bedridden with a broken leg for more than two weeks.

5. No one can put up with his bad temper, not even his family.

6-1. You'd do the same if you were in my place. 或 Were you in my place, you'd do the same.

6-2. If I'd been born（或Had I been born）in the US, I'd be able to speak fluent English.

7. For the poor, he had no compassion whatsoever.

8. You need to bring his attention to the fact that the public opinion is not in his favor.

9. Our lives seem to have gotten better since we moved here. 或 Since moving here, our lives seem to have improved.

10. It just so happens that we have exactly the part you're looking for.

11. It is unlikely that the polar ice caps will melt away.

12. We spent the remainder of our vacation visiting museums and shopping.

13. I was at a loss as to where to seek for help.

14. Just as I had expected, the news turned out to be very encouraging.

15. I thought she'd be a little tired after running the race, but to my surprise, she was still bursting with energy.

16. Without Internet access, I have no way of knowing which restaurant serves the best beef noodles.

17. I couldn't resist kissing the baby's adorable face.

18-1. Considering the age at which he won the Nobel prize, we ought to respect him even more.

18-2. Our family will have to scrimp and save to be able to afford a new computer.

19. He hungers for the opportunity to serve his country.

The Lilacs in the Valley
山谷裡的丁香花

1-5　　我的家世世代代都住在這個小村莊裡，村莊坐落在山谷裡，山谷裡有一大片草原，草原邊緣長滿了丁香樹，春天裡，草原周圍開滿了淡紫色的丁香花，山谷裡也到處都飄散著花香。

　　我們孩子們一有空，就在草原上玩，我們這些鄉下孩子，除了自己家和學校以外，幾乎大半時間都在這個草原上度過。

　　一年前，有人來告訴爸爸，說政府徵兵，他應該立刻入伍，爸爸只好吻別了我們全家人，下山去了。一開始還有信來，半年前，消息斷了，媽媽去打聽，得到的消息是，爸爸在戰場上失蹤了。

　　我們附近的鄰居中的叔叔伯伯們，都去打仗了，村子裡只剩下一些老弱婦孺，我們這些男孩子們，除了在草原上玩以外，還要做一些田裡的粗活。

　　我去問老師，究竟爸爸去打誰？老師告訴我，他們是去打回教徒，我追問為什麼要打回教徒，老師似乎答不上來，他說的理由好像與歷史有關，顯然四百年前的一些怨怨恨恨，到今天又被舊事重提了。

CD1-9
◇ generation (n.) 世代
◇ border (v.) 相接；毗連
◇ abundance (n.) 豐盛；大量
◇ fragrance (n.) 芳香
◇ drift (v.) (此處指花香) 飄 (散)

◇ conscript (v.) 徵召 (入伍)
◇ immediately (adv.) 即刻地；立即地
◇ conscript (v.) 徵召 (入伍)
◇ immediately (adv.) 即刻地；立即地
◇ Muslim ['mʌzləm] (n.) 回教徒

My family has lived in this village for generations. The village
is situated in a valley with a large, grassy meadow bordered by an
abundance of lilac trees. In the spring, the area around the meadow
is filled with light purple lilac blossoms, and their fragrance drifts
throughout the valley.

Whenever we kids have nothing to do, we play in the meadow.
Other than home and school, that's where we spend most of our time.

A year ago, someone came to tell my dad that the government
was conscripting soldiers, which meant that he had to join the army
immediately. So Dad was forced to kiss us all goodbye and leave our
mountain home. At first there were letters, but six months ago they
stopped coming. Mom asked around, and the news she got was that
Dad had gone missing in action.

All the grown men from our neighborhood had gone to war, so our
village was left with only women, children, the old and the weak.
Besides just playing on the grass, we boys had to start doing some
hard work in the fields as well.

I asked my teacher who exactly it was that my dad had gone to
fight against. Teacher told me we were fighting the Muslims. I asked
her why we were fighting the Muslims, but she didn't seem to have
an answer. The reason she mentioned had something to do with
history—apparently some old resentments from four hundred years
ago had flared up again somehow.

◇ resentment(n.)憎恨
◇ flare(v.)閃焰(此處片語 flare up 指的是戰事「突然發生」)

6-10　　有一天,有一個砲兵的部隊開進了村子,他們將大砲架在山谷裡的草原上,也架了很多的壕溝,造了掩體,他們的到來,使我們男孩子大為興奮,成天看這些兵士們操演,第一次演習放砲的時候,我們都在遠處大聲的歡呼。

　　我從未看過回教徒,只知道幾十年來,我們基督徒一直和他們和樂相處,為什麼忽然又要打起來了,我始終弄不清楚。

　　終於,我們開火了,砲兵們在一天清晨忽然向山下開砲,我們從熟睡中被吵醒,砲不僅吵醒了我們,也幾乎震破了我們的窗子,媽媽馬上將我們聚合在一起,躲在一張桌子下面。

　　兩天以後,對方反擊了,砲彈零零星星地落在村子各地,幾乎沒有損害到砲兵的基地。可是我們的好日子沒有了,一聽到砲聲,我們就要找一個地方躲一下。

　　有一個晚上,回教徒的砲彈非常精確地落在草原砲兵基地上,我們的砲兵還來不及回手,大砲就在一小時內幾乎被摧毀了。士兵失去了

◇ rumble(v.)轟隆隆作響　　　　◇ drill(v.)演習;演練
◇ trench(n.)壕溝　　　　　　　　◇ cannon(n.)大砲;加農砲
◇ bunker(n.)碉堡　　　　　　　　◇ Christian(n.)基督徒

One day an artillery unit rumbled into our village. They set up
their big guns in the meadow of our valley, dug lots of trenches and
built bunkers. Their arrival was quite an exciting event for us boys.
For days on end we watched the soldiers drill. The first time they
practiced firing their cannons, we cheered loudly from a safe distance.

I'd never seen a Muslim before—I only knew that for the past few
decades, we Christians had gotten along with them just fine. Why
were we fighting each other all of a sudden? I never did get it figured
out.

Eventually, battle broke out. The artillerymen suddenly began
firing their guns down from the mountain early one morning, jarring
us awake. The guns didn't just wake us up—they practically shattered
our windows. Mom rushed to gather us all together, and we huddled
under a table for shelter.

Two days later, the enemy counterattacked. Their shells fell
haphazardly all over the village, leaving the artillery soldiers' base
almost completely undamaged. Nevertheless, our good days were
over—whenever we heard shelling, we would have to find a place to
hide.

Then one night, the Muslim bombs fell with devastating accuracy

6-10

◇ jar (v.) 發出尖銳刺耳的雜聲
◇ shatter (v.) 震碎；粉碎
◇ huddle (v.) 擠；瑟縮
◇ counterattack (v.) 反擊；反攻

◇ shell (n.) 砲彈
◇ base (n.) 基地；陣地
◇ devastating (adj.) 摧殘的；毀滅的；重
　創的

大砲，只好撤退，他們不僅沒有砲，連一輛車子也沒有，所有的人都要步行下山。

11-15　部隊長帶了一位傷兵到我的家，這位可憐的叔叔變成了盲人，腿也斷了。雖然他只有輕聲的呻吟，我們可以想像得到他有多大的痛苦。部隊顯然沒有什麼醫藥可以減少他的痛苦，部隊長請媽媽照顧這位年輕人，他說戰爭一有轉機，他們就會回來帶他去就醫。他們用擔架抬他進入我們的房子，媽媽立刻答應收留他，也保證會讓他和我們一起生活，我們吃什麼，他也會吃什麼，不會虧待他的。

年輕人的夥伴們向他殷殷道別，臨走還給他一支手槍，他接過以後放在枕頭下面。

雖然部隊撤退了，我們仍聽到砲聲，我們已很有經驗，大概知道放的地方有多遠，敵人離我們越來越近了。

媽媽問這位年輕人的姓名和他家的地址，因為媽媽想也許可以設法

◇ destroy (v.) 摧毀；毀滅　　　　◇ commander (n.) 指揮官
◇ retreat (v.) 撤退；後退　　　　◇ blind (v.) 使 (人) 眼瞎
◇ descend [dɪˋsɛnd] (v.) 下降；降低　◇ groan (v.) 呻吟

on the artillerymen's base in the meadow. Our soldiers had no time to strike back; almost all their cannons were destroyed within an hour. Without their big guns, they were forced to retreat. Not only did they have no artillery, but they didn't have a single vehicle, either—they all had to descend the mountain on foot.

Their commander brought a wounded soldier to our house. The poor fellow had been blinded, and his leg was broken, too. Although he only groaned quietly, we could imagine how much pain he must be in. The commander appeared not to have any drugs to dull his pain. He asked Mom to take care of the young man, promising that they'd come back and take him to a hospital as soon as the war started going better. They carried him into our house on a stretcher; right away Mom agreed to take him in. She promised that he would live together with us, eat what we ate, and be treated as one of our own.

The young man's comrades bid him a melancholy farewell. Just before they left, they gave him a handgun, which he put under his pillow.

Although the troops had retreated, we could still hear the sounds of artillery. By now we were experienced enough to know how far away the shelling was. The enemy was getting closer.

Mom asked the young man for his name and home address, as she thought we might be able to find a way to let his family know he was

11-15

◇ stretcher (n.) 擔架
◇ treat (v.) 對待；醫治
◇ melancholy (adj.) 哀傷的；憂怨的
◇ experienced (adj.) 經驗豐富的
◇ shelling (n.) 砲擊

讓他家人知道他仍活著，他怎麼都不肯讓我們知道，他說反正失蹤的人多的是，就讓他家人以為他失蹤了算了。

媽媽聽了以後，偷偷地哭了一場，這位年輕人不知道我爸爸也已經失蹤了。

16-20 已是春天，草原上的丁香花開了。在屋子裡都可以聞到丁香花的香味。

有一天，天氣好得不得了，天特別地藍，年輕人問我們是不是外面天氣很好。我們說是的。他懇求我們抬他到草原上去，那天一聲砲都沒有，我們幾個小孩子七手八腳地將他抬了出去。他又問我們是不是丁香花開了。我們說是的。他要求我們將他放在一棵丁香樹的下面，也叫我們採一大把丁香花給他。

然後，他叫我們小孩子到草原上玩，只是不要靠近砲，因為仍有爆炸的可能。他說他要在丁香花下睡一下。

我和哥哥帶著我們家的牧羊犬在草原上追逐，忽然我們聽到一聲槍響，我們趕快跑回去，發現年輕人的槍掉在地上，我們採的花也散落了一地。

◇ persuade（v.）勸；說服
◇ blossom（v.）開花
◇ scent（n.）芳香；香氣
◇ entreat（v.）懇求
◇ clumsily（adv.）笨手笨腳地；笨拙地
◇ bloom（n.）花（此處和 in 形成片語 in bloom，表示「花朵盛開」）
◇ explode（v.）爆炸

still alive. But nothing could persuade him to tell us. "In any case," he said, "plenty of people have disappeared in this war—just let them think that I'm one of them."

After she heard him say that, Mom went off alone and cried. The young man didn't know that my dad had disappeared too.

Spring came, and the lilacs in the meadow blossomed. The sweet scent drifted everywhere, indoors and out.

16-20
CD1-8

On one particularly lovely day, when the sky was especially blue, the young man asked us if it was a beautiful day. When we said that it was, he entreated us to carry him out to the meadow. It was a quiet day, without a single sound of shelling. Several of us kids teamed up rather clumsily to carry him out. He asked whether the lilacs were in bloom, and we told him they were. "Put me under a lilac tree," he said, "and pick a big handful of lilacs for me."

Then he told us to go play in the meadow, but make sure we stayed away from the shells, for it was still possible that they might explode. He said he wanted to sleep for a while under the lilacs.

My brother and I took our sheep dogs out to the meadow and chased each other around. All of a sudden we heard a gunshot. We ran back as fast as we could. There we found the young man's gun where it had fallen to the ground. The blossoms we picked had scattered everywhere.

◇ gunshot(n.)槍擊(聲)　　　　◇ scatter(v.)散開；散落

　　媽媽說我們該趕快將他埋葬起來，可是不可能找到棺材了。媽媽動員了很多人，挖了一個長方形的墓穴，媽媽用床單將年輕人包了起來，也準備了一床毯子，準備將他放進泥土以後，用毯子把他蓋好。她說這樣年輕人的嘴裡才不至於吃到泥土。

21-25　　因為都要靠我們這些小孩子挖洞，洞挖好已是黃昏。村裡的老神父到了，他請人將教堂的鐘打了起來。

　　自從戰爭爆發以來，這還是第一次教堂打鐘。

　　在我們要將擔架放下去的時候，一些回教徒的士兵出現了，他們悄悄地進入了村子，小心翼翼地前進。當他們看到我們不用棺材埋葬的時候，都露出訝異的表情，其中有一位是軍官的人問我們，「他是回教徒嗎？」

　　後來我才知道，回教徒不用棺材的，他們只是將屍體用布包起來埋掉，讓死去的人早日回歸自然。

　　我們告訴軍官，我們沒有棺材，只好如此，軍官低低地自言自語，「想不到死亡使我們都一樣了。」他叫他的部下脫下帽子，在旁邊觀

◇ coffin（n.）棺木　　　　　　◇ grave（n.）墳；墓穴
◇ mobilize（v.）動員　　　　　◇ priest（n.）牧師

Mom said we should bury him quickly, but we couldn't find a coffin. So she mobilized a group of people to dig a rectangular grave, wrapped the young man in a bedsheet and prepared a blanket to cover him with after he was lowered into the ground. That way, she said, the young man wouldn't get dirt in his mouth.

Since the only people around to dig the grave were us children, it was evening by the time we finished. The village priest came by and asked someone to go ring the bell in the chapel.

21-25

It was the first time the chapel bell had tolled since the war broke out.

As we were about to lower the stretcher into the grave, some Muslim soldiers appeared. They had silently entered the village and were cautiously advancing. When they saw that we were burying someone without a coffin, their expressions showed great surprise. One of their officers asked us, "Is he a Muslim?"

Only later did I discover that Muslims don't use coffins—they just wrap the body in cloth and bury it so the dead man (or woman) will return to nature more quickly.

We told the officer that since we didn't have a coffin, this was the best we could do. "Never realized how death makes us all the

---

◇ chapel (n.) (小型)教堂　　　　　　◇ cautiously (adv.)謹慎地；小心地
◇ toll (v.) (鐘)響；鳴

禮。我們幾個男孩子負責填土，因為是小孩子，進度很慢，還是靠一些回教徒的士兵將土填了回去。

26-28　　這是兩週以前的事，年輕人的墓地由於春雨的滋潤而長滿了草。丁香花謝了以後，都會落在這塊新的草地上，我們沒有做任何的記號，只有我們知道，這裡埋葬了一個年輕人。

　　回教士兵走了以後，我們的小村莊不再聽到砲聲，我們小孩子上課、種田也恢復了在草原上互相盡情地追逐玩耍。可是，我相信，我們這些男孩子都有一個共同的想法：總有一天，有些大人要將我們送上戰場，我們都可能永遠回不來了。

　　可是我仍有一個小小的願望，我希望我們國家裡到處都種滿了丁香花的樹，如果我不能回來，我希望能被埋在丁香花樹下面。春天來的時候，讓淡紫色的丁香花灑在我的身上。

◇ murmur (v.) 模糊地說；喃喃而語
◇ subordinate (n.) 部下
◇ ceremony (n.) 儀式；典禮
◇ progress (n.) 進度；進展
◇ patch (n.)（一）片；（一）塊
◇ mark (v.) 標示；作記號

same," the officer murmured to himself. He told his subordinates to take off their hats and watch the ceremony. I and a few other boys were responsible for filling in the hole; since we were just kids, our progress was very slow. We ended up relying on some of the Muslim soldiers to fill in the grave.

This happened two weeks ago. Since then, the young man's grave has been watered by the spring rain, and it is now covered in grass. After the lilacs wilt, they'll fall on this new patch of grass. We didn't mark the grave at all—we're the only ones who know there's a young man buried there.　　**26-28**

After the Muslim soldiers left, our village no longer heard the sounds of artillery. We children went to school, worked in the fields and reverted to our old habits of playing and chasing each other around the meadow to our heart's content. But I believe there is one thought that we boys all share: sooner or later, a day will come when some grownups will send us off to war, and we may not ever come back again.

But I still have a small wish: I wish that every corner of our country was planted full of lilac trees. If I don't make it back, I hope I can be buried underneath one of them so that when spring comes, the light purple blossoms will sprinkle over my body.

◇ revert (v.) 回復；重返
◇ content (n.) 快足；飽滿
◇ light (adj.) 淡的
◇ sprinkle (v.) 灑落

(1) an abundance of... 大量的……；豐盛的……(1段)

The village is situated in a valley with a large, grassy meadow bordered by an abundance of lilac trees.

村莊坐落在山谷裡，山谷裡有一大片草原，草原邊緣長滿了丁香樹。

解析

abundance 本身為「大量」、「豐富」的意思，由此字所形成的片語 an abundance of，當然也脫離不了這方面的意思。讀者要留心的是，這個片語和另一個片語 plenty of 一樣，可以指不可數的東西，如 plenty of confidence，同時也可以指可數的東西，如 plenty of high-rises。

在原英譯裡，另有兩個值得注意的要點，一個為 is situated「坐落在……」、「位置在……」。

◇ 整個城市坐落在一個盆地裡。
The whole city is situated in a basin.

另一個要點為 bordered by...，它的意思為「有……環繞其周邊」。

◇ 村落的三面為一條小溪所環繞。
Three sides of the village are bordered by a creek.

小試身手

1. 農夫們收成豐盛，都說今年真是個好年頭。

_____

---

(2) other than... 扣除……不算(2段)

Other than home and school, that's where we spend most of our time.

除了自己家和學校以外，(我們)幾乎大半時間都在這個草原上度過。

解析

如果你有個非常非常文靜內向的朋友,除了家人和兩個好朋友,他幾乎不和其他人講話,即使學校老師也是,你就可以說:

Other than his parents and one or two friends, he never talks to anybody else, not even his teachers.

你這位非常非常文靜內向的朋友除了吃飯接好友電話,都把自己關在房間裡。這時候你得說:

Other than coming down to meals or to take phone calls, he shuts himself in his room all day.

小試身手

2. 除了直升機,沒有其他交通工具可以帶你到那裡。

_____

---

(3) missing in action 作戰失蹤(3段)

Mom asked around, and the news she got was that Dad had gone missing in action.

媽媽去打聽,得到的消息是,爸爸在戰場上失蹤了。

解析

不管理由有多充分,不管口號有多崇高,不管是為私利而輕啟戰端或者是為生存而迎戰,多少文明因而遭到摧毀,多少家庭因而破碎。請記住,戰爭是理性的人類所進行的最不理性的行為,戰爭永遠是殘酷的。無論是侵入攻擊的一方,或者保家土的一方,總有人 KIA(= killed in action 作戰死亡);有人 MIA(= missing in action 作戰失蹤);也有人為對方所俘,變成 POW(= prisoner of war 戰俘)。

英譯裡另有一個片語 asked around，它的意思為「四處問」、「到處打聽」。

◇ 最近有個人四處在打聽你的住處。
Somebody has been asking around about where you live.

小試身手

3. 一個調查(investigation)小組成立(organize)來搜集更多關於作戰失
蹤者的事實。

_____

（4）have something to do with... 與……有關（5段）
flare up 燃起

The reason she mentioned had something to do with history—
apparently some old resentments from four hundred years ago had flared
up again somehow.

他說的理由好像與歷史有關，顯然四百年前的一些怨怨恨恨，到今天又
被舊事重提了。

解析

我們從最基本的片語 have to do with... 出發，它的意思為「有關係」。如果
我們利用這個片語，添加不同的字，就會有不同程度的「關係」出來：

「大有關係」：have a lot to do with...
「有點關係；頗有關係」：have something to do with
「沒什麼關係」：have little to do with
「毫無關係」：have nothing to do with

另外的一個值得學習的東西為 flare up 這個片語。也許你曾有過生火烤肉的經驗，在火熄了之後，灰燼其實仍在燜燒，一有機會，比如對它吹一口氣，或者撥動一下，可能火苗又會短暫閃現，flare up 就在表達這種情形。四百年前的恩怨，就像殘火餘燼，表面看似快飛灰湮滅，其實一經撩撥，就有可能再度死灰復燃（即中文原著所謂「舊事重提」）。往事不堪回首，舊事豈可重提。舊事一經重提，眼前的新仇再加上心頭的舊恨，不是又一起同時湧現了嗎？

小試身手

4. 謠傳說他被綁架和鉅額債務頗有關係。

_____

---

(5) for days on end 一連好幾天（6段）

For days on end we watched the soldiers drill.
（我們）成天看著這些兵士們操演。

解析

for days on end 是譯者對於中文「成天」的詮釋，不曉得你的看法如何？或許在你的看法裡，「成天」就是「整天」、「一天到晚」的意思，所以你想用來詮釋，那當然沒什麼問題。可是如果你仔細思量一下，「成天」從某個角度來思考，也的確有譯者所認為的「一連好幾天」意思。

小試身手

5. 每天晚上，她坐在書桌前連讀好幾小時的書。

_____

（6）get along with someone just fine 和某人相處得不差（7段）

I only knew that for the past few decades, we Christians had gotten along with them just fine.

（我）只知道幾十年來，我們基督徒一直和他們和樂相處。

解析

當然我們得先對 get along 有個了解，這個片語的基本含意為「相處」，所以「他們處不來。」英文就是：They don't get along. 反之，如果他們相處得很融洽，就是：They get along well(with each other). 原譯文裡的 we Christians had gotten along with them just fine，裡頭有個 just fine，約相當於中文「還不錯」、「過得去」。唉，基督徒和回教徒能處到 just fine 這個程度，也可算是「和樂融融」了，你同意否？

小試身手

6.　他從來就和他一起共事的人處不好。

_____

（7）jar someone awake（巨響或刺耳的聲音）把某人（從睡夢中）驚醒（8段）

The artillerymen suddenly began firing their guns down from the mountain early one morning, jarring us awake.

砲兵們在一天清晨忽然向山下開砲，我們從熟睡中被吵醒。

解析

jar 在這裡為動詞，意思是「震動」、「刺激」。為了升學讀書真是件苦事，三更燈火五更雞，每天能小憩休息的時間實在不多。許多學子們往往熬不住才往床上一躺，躺下去以後又往往累得爬不起床，即使床榻邊的鬧鐘鳴叫不已，也起不了作用，上學在即，這可怎麼辦？老爸老媽儘管心疼，也只好連

搖帶晃地把未來的龍鳳喚醒。請看以下的例句：

◈ 要不是我母親及時把我搖醒，我現在可能還在家裡睡覺。
If my mom hadn't shaken me awake in time, I might still be asleep at home right now.

把人搖醒英文為 shake somebody awake，那麼噪音聲響把人吵醒就要使用 jar somebody awake 了。

小試身手

7. 隔壁傳過來的重金屬音樂的轟轟聲把我從睡夢中吵醒好幾次。

_____

---

(8) leave... undamaged 沒有造成損害（9段）

Their shells fell haphazardly all over the village, leaving the artillery soldiers' base almost completely undamaged.
砲彈零零星星地落在村子各地，幾乎沒有損害到砲兵的基地。

解析

讀者要花些心思和力氣來了解這個重要的結構：在主要事件發生後，呈現了什麼樣子的影響或造成了什麼樣的結果，以英文言就是：S+V+... , leaving...

現在我們試著化理論為實際，設定一個主要事件和一個結果或影響。

主要事件：暴雨終於停了
結果或影響：（造成）整個都市泡在水中
整句：暴雨終於停了，（造成）整個都市泡在水中。
英文：The rainstorm finally let up, leaving the whole town drenched in water.
再看一例如何？

主要事件：炸彈爆炸了
結果或影響：（造成）幾十個人死亡、幾百個人受傷
整句：炸彈爆炸了，（造成）幾十個人死亡、幾百個人受傷。
英文：The bomb exploded, leaving scores of people dead and hundreds
　　　wounded.

小試身手

8. 火很快就自行熄滅，大部分的家具都沒有受損。

_____

---

(9) dull one's pain 減輕痛苦（11段）

The commander appeared not to have any drugs to dull his pain.

部隊顯然沒有什麼醫藥可以減少他的痛苦。

解析

如果你想要表達「我左手肘隱隱作痛」，該怎麼說呢？對啦，dull 正是你所需要的字眼，你可說：I've got a dull pain in my left elbow. 在這個句子裡，dull 是形容詞，表示疼痛的程度是「隱約的」、「暗暗的」，疼痛的確存在，但是感覺並不那麼強烈。若你想要表達很痛，痛得不得了，那你可以把 dull 換成 sharp 或 severe 或 acute 等字。(dull 的本意是「鈍」，而 sharp 則是「利」。)

不過，在原英譯中，dull 的作用是動詞，綜合上一段的說明，讀者應該很容易想見，dull 的意思是「把痛楚的感覺降低或抑制」。使用它一方面很口語，另方面很傳神，因為它把明顯而強烈的痛楚降低減緩到「隱約的」或「暗暗的」的程度了。英文表示「止痛」用 kill the pain 表示；「減輕疼痛」用 lessen the pain，而 dull the pain 的地位則似乎很介於這極口語和正式用字兩者之間。

小試身手

9. 他在我疼痛的肩部肌肉噴上某種東西，它的止／減痛效果很好。

_____

(10) bid someone farewell 向（某人）道別（12段）

The young man's comrades bid him a melancholy farewell.
年輕人的夥伴們向他殷殷道別。

解析

首先請讀者們注意到動詞 bid 的不規則變化。大概一般人都知道它是不規則動詞，原形動詞 ― 過去式動詞 ― 過去分詞的變化式為：bid ― bade ― bidden；可是它也可以作 bid ― bid ― bidden 的變化，這可能是一般讀者們比較不熟悉的。所以，親愛的讀者，別懷疑譯者把動詞搞錯了，譯文裡的 bid 的確是過去式動詞，相當於一般人比較熟悉的另一個過去式形式 bade。

中文裡有「道」早安、「道」別／再見之類的說法，就英文而言，就可以用動詞 bid 一以概之。所以，你當然可以說 bid good morning/ bid goodbye，而且在使用上常使用 bid someone good-bye 或 bid good-bye to someone 的形式。

小試身手

10. 他抓著我的手，向我道別，然後登上火車。

_____

（11） ask somebody for something 向（某人）索討（某物）（14段）

Mom asked the young man for his name and home address, as she thought we might be able to find a way to let his family know he was still alive.

媽媽問這位年輕人的姓名和他家的地址，因為媽媽想也許可以設法讓他家人知道他仍活著。

解析

究其實，片語 ask for 的最基本含義為「索討」、「要求」，比如「我要求一個更詳細的說明。」英文為 I asked for a more detailed explanation. 若是想要說明索討或要求的對象，則可以把這對象安置在動詞 ask 之後使之成為 ask someone for something 的形式。你媽媽有一手烤蛋糕的絕活，不少人都向她要秘方。英文就可以說：My mother bakes a delicious cake. Lots of people have asked her for the recipe.

小試身手

11. 我請求他允許（permission）我使用傳真機（fax machine）。

_____

（12） team up 合起來；團結起來（17段）

Several of us kids teamed up rather clumsily to carry him out.

我們幾個小孩七手八腳地將他抬了出去。

解析

即使高明的譯者，碰上「七手八腳」，恐怕也要傷神好一陣子吧。譯者利用片語 teamed up 再配上副詞 clumsily（笨拙地）就把它詮釋出來了，這片語

的本意不難從字面看出：「組織成一個團隊」，比如你給某人忠告：「這是件難得不得了的工作。你需要和他團隊合作才可望成功。」英文可以表達為：This is an extraordinarily difficult task. You'll need to team up with him in order to succeed.

反面來說，如果一群狐群狗黨不走正路，專門欺壓善良，這樣的一夥人，英文名之為 gang。把這個字當成動詞使用，和 up 結合起來，也可以形成一個片語，這裡舉個例子把它靈活運用：「他們結夥來欺壓他並偷了他的錢。」英文為：They ganged up on him and stole his money.

小試身手

12. 我們非合作不可，因為那不是個人獨力 (single-handedly) 所能辦到的事。

_____

（13）in bloom（花）開（17段）

He asked whether the lilacs were in bloom.
他又問我們是不是丁香花開了。

解析

The flowers are in bloom. 意為「花兒正開著」。若要強調「盛開」可以 in full bloom 表達。bloom 多以動詞型態出現，所以本句也可譯為 He asked whether the lilacs were blooming.

小試身手

13. 成千上萬的遊客到陽明山觀賞各式各樣盛開的花朵。

_____

（14）a big handful of... 一大把……東西（17段）

"Put me under a lilac tree," he said, "and pick a big handful of lilacs for me."

他要求我們將他放在一棵丁香樹的下面，也叫我們採一大把丁香花給他。

解析

首先讀者要知道這個 handful 雖然怎麼看都像形容詞（-ful），其實它是名詞。人體部位的一些名詞常被應用在這樣的情況裡，讀者可以看以下的例子：ear → earful；mouth → mouthful；arm → armful；lung → lungful。

其實再加上了 -ful 之後，已經不是指那個身體部位了，而是指和那個部位有關的「量」，而且是很大的量，至少就那個部位的標準來看確是如此。所以，mouthful 的基本含意為「滿滿一大口」，armful 的基本含意為「滿滿一懷抱」lungful 的基本含意為「滿滿一肺部」。那你猜猜看，earful 是什麼意思？我們把這兩個字的用法設計成小試身手的練習，讀者不妨親身體驗看看。

男性讀者們，有心儀的對象嗎？惦惦自己的荷包，衡量自己的財力，考慮送她「一束花」a bunch of flowers，或「一大把花」a handful of flowers，或「一大捧花」an armful of flowers，聽說效果很不錯哦。

小試身手

14-1. 他捧起滿手的沙，再讓它們從指尖滑落。

_____

14-2. 我聽夠了她了無新意的教訓，逐漸不耐煩起來。

_____

（15）all of a sudden 猛然間；突然（19段）

All of a sudden we heard a gunshot.

忽然我們聽到一聲槍響。

解析

sudden 本來常作形容詞，可是置身在這個片語裡，它卻是不折不扣當名詞使用（請特別注意，它前面還有個冠詞 a），而且當名詞用時，也幾乎只用在這個片語。a sudden 意思為「一件突如其來的事情」，因此，all of a sudden 幾個字的組合，就傳達出「完全在那一陣突然之間」的字面含意，對學習英文的人而言，如果從這角度去看這個片語，應該會覺得還好，不算難記難學，而它就相當於 suddenly 這個副詞。

> **小試身手**
>
> 15. 突然間風勢增強（rise）而海面起浪（rough）。
>
> _____

（16）若干個要點解析（20段）

So she mobilized a group of people to dig a rectangular grave, wrapped the young man in a bedsheet and prepared a blanket to cover him with after he was lowered into the ground.

媽媽（她）動員了很多人，挖了一個長方形的墓穴，媽媽用床單將年輕人包了起來，也準備了一床毯子，準備將他放進泥土以後，用毯子把他蓋好。

解析

幾何圖形的英文說法，常見的有長方形、正方形、三角形。它們的英文分別為 rectangle/ square/ triangle，而它們的形容詞則分別為 rectangular/ square/ triangular。

其次來看看 to cover... with，with 這個介詞的出現會讓一些學習英文的人很不適應。到底這是怎麼回事呢？請各位先思考以下的句子：他丟支筆讓我簽名使用。

你會如何以英文來表現這句話呢？如果你的答案如下，那就相當不錯了。
◇He tossed me a pen with which I could sign my name.

如果你的答案如下，請不要緊張，那也是正確的。
◇He tossed me a pen that I could write my name with.

現在我們把上句個小手術，把 that I could write my name with 這麼個一身贅肉的身軀瘦身減肥為 to write my name with，也就是把子句 (that...) 化簡為不定詞 (to write...)。至於在精減的過程中，什麼東西去掉了，什麼東西加進來了，就勞駕各位費神觀察思考一番，這一層工夫省不得，也只有透過自己 DIY，才會生出心得。

小試身手

16. 我沒有可以依靠的人。

_____

（17）end up Ving... 到最後……；到頭來……（25段）

We ended up relying on some of the Muslim soldiers to fill in the grave.
(我們)還是靠一些回教徒的士兵將土填了回去。

解析

end 作動詞用，本身即帶有「結束」、「終結」的意思，因此，end up Ving... 的基本含意為「以……為終結」，也就是「到頭來……」的意思。中文諺語說「少壯不努力，老大徒傷悲。」此言即是，年輕時候，讀書也好、

做事也好，總是以勤奮上進為宜，否則韶華易逝，等年紀老大時，落得街頭乞討為生（end up begging for charity on the street）的下場，情何以堪呢？

若 end up 之後不是跟隨一個動作，而是一個事件或活動（以名詞表示），這時候需要在 end up 的後面添加介詞 in，再接該名詞，小試身手裡的練習即是。

小試身手

17. 比賽最後因為有爭議的一分（disputed point）而打架收場。

_____

（18）make it back（活著）回來（28段）

If I don't make it back, I hope I can be buried underneath one of them...
如果我不能回來，我希望能被埋在丁香花樹下面。

解析

這是一個純粹的慣用語，以 make it back 來表示「回來」，並且帶有「活著回來」的意味，是個很活潑、很生活化的句子。這樣的句子可以靈活運用，比如你進新竹或宜蘭，離台北不算太遠，你可以說：I can make it back to Taipei before dark.「我可以在天黑前回到台北。」

若是要去聽哪位歌手或哪個樂團的演唱會，看到父母為難的表情，你大可向他們說：「放心，我會在半夜前安全回到家的。」：No need to worry, I'll make it back home before midnight.

曾經想像過，不搭電梯，徒步爬到世界第一高樓頂，要花多少時間嗎？以下這位老兄二十分鐘就辦到了。
◇He made it up to the top floor of Taipei 101 on foot in twenty minutes.

小試身手

18. 他冒著狂風大雨的天候游回到岸上。(註:在此句裡,made it back to shore其實不一定指「游回」岸上,也可能是把船「開回」岸邊。)

_____

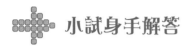 小試身手解答

1. The farmers had an abundance of crops and said it was a real good year.

2. Other than a helicopter, there's not any means of transportation to take you there.

3. An investigation team was organized to gather more information about those missing in action.

4. His kidnapping is rumored to have something to do with his huge debts.

5. Every evening she sits at her desk and studies for hours on end.

6. He has never got along with anyone working with him.

7. The booming sound of heavy metal music coming from next door jarred me awake several times.

8. The fire quickly burned itself out, leaving most of the furniture undamaged.

9. He sprayed something on my aching shoulder muscles and it worked wonderfully to dull the pain.

10. He took my hands in his, bade me farewell and got on the train.

11. I asked him for permission to use the fax machine.

12. We had to team up because it was not something that could be done

single-handedly.

13. Thousands and thousands of visitors go to Yangmingshan to enjoy the sight of all kinds of flowers in full bloom.

14-1. He scooped up a handful of sand and let it run through between his fingers.

14-2. I had had an earful of her meaningless preaching and was beginning to feel impatient.

15. All of a sudden the wind rose and the sea got rough.

16. I have no one to rely on. (I have no one on whom I can rely.)

17. The game ended up in a fight over a disputed point.

18. He made it back to shore in extremely stormy weather.

I Love Black Drongos
我愛烏秋

1-5　　在所有的鳥類中，我現在最愛烏秋，一種貌不驚人的黑鳥，比麻雀要大，可是又比烏鴉小，全身漆黑，除了體形比烏鴉小以外，其餘都像烏鴉。

　　五年前吧，有一天我騎腳踏車去清華校園，走出車棚，忽然感到一隻鳥從我的後面飛過去，而且距離我的頭只有幾寸，這隻鳥飛到我前面的一棵樹上，先是用非常好聽的聲音叫了一陣子，然後又對我俯衝下來，這次我看得一清二楚，牠俯衝的架式就像老式戰鬥機俯衝投彈一模一樣。牠以我為目標，到達我頭上以後，又拉起鳥頭，揚長而去。

　　我記得非常清楚，這隻烏秋攻擊我的日子大約在六月初，不久就是學生畢業了。

　　大約有兩個星期左右，幾隻烏秋鳥專門在清華園的交通要道對行人俯衝攻擊，有一兩位甚至被鳥爪抓到，氣得半死。

　　我注意到這些鳥從不攻擊女性，牠們似乎最恨男孩子，尤其是小男

CD2-2

◇ harmless (adj.) 無害的
◇ sparrow (n.) 麻雀
◇ crow [kro] (n.) 烏鴉
◇ pitch black 烏黑；漆黑
◇ appearance (n.) 外表；外貌
◇ distinguish (v.) 區別；分辨

◇ campus (n.) 校園
◇ bike shed 腳踏車棚
◇ perch (v.) 棲息；駐留
◇ swoop (v.) 俯衝；飛撲
◇ fighter plane 戰鬥機
◇ target (n.) 靶子；目標

Of all the birds in the world, I now love black drongos the best. A black drongo is a kind of harmless-looking black bird, bigger than a sparrow but smaller than a crow. Its whole body is pitch black, and besides its smaller size, nothing about its appearance distinguishes it from a crow.

1-5 CD2-1

About five years ago, I rode my bicycle to the Tsing Hua campus one day. After I walked out of the bike shed, I suddenly felt a bird fly over me from behind, a mere few inches from my head. The bird perched in a tree in front of me, where it sang beautifully for a while, then abruptly swooped down on me again. This time I clearly saw that the way it dove was exactly like how old fighter planes used to dive-bomb. It locked onto me like a target; then, as it reached my head, it pulled up and flew away, looking very pleased with itself.

I distinctly remember that the day the drongo attacked me was around the beginning of June, just before graduation.

For about two weeks, a few black drongos took it upon themselves to dive at pedestrians along the main thoroughfares of the Tsing Hua campus. There were even a couple people who got scratched by the birds' claws, to their extreme displeasure.

I noticed that the birds never attacked women. It was as though

◇ pleased (adj.) 得意的；愉快的
◇ distinctly (adv.) 清晰地；分明地
◇ attack (v.) 攻擊
◇ graduation (n.) 畢業
◇ pedestrian [pəˋdɛstrɪən] (n.) 路人；行人
◇ thoroughfare [ˋθɝoˏfɛr] (n.) 大路；通道
◇ scratch (v.) 抓傷
◇ claw (n.) (鳥類的) 爪
◇ displeasure (n.) 不悅；不高興

孩，這些頑童一來，牠們一定來攻擊。最奇怪的是，牠們攻擊以前，
一概先發出極為可愛的叫聲。

6-10　　有些男孩子甚為不服，會在地上撿起石子還擊，我有一次被牠惹火
了，也曾還擊，路過的一群學生，看到我返老還童，用石頭打鳥，認
為極為有趣，對我指指點點，我當時已是世界上最偉大的教授，為了
保持大教授的尊嚴，只好忍氣吞聲，讓烏秋攻擊而不還手。

　　以後每年六月，烏秋就會對行人（多半是男人）展開攻擊，為什麼選
這個時間，至今是個謎。有一次我陪一位大官參觀校園，這些大官道
貌岸然，十分莊嚴，偏偏烏秋不識相，對準了他俯衝而來，大官一慌
之下，蹲了下去。需知大人物是不可以如此失態的，雖然我們大家全
體假裝沒有看見，他已是大丟其臉，我們以後再也不必太尊敬他了。

◇ grudge（n.）仇；怨　　　　　　　◇ goad（v.）惹火
◇ miscreant [ˈmɪskrɪənt]（n.）壞蛋　◇ childish（adj.）孩子氣的
◇ lovely（adj.）可愛的　　　　　　◇ professor（n.）教授
◇ defeat（n.）打敗；擊敗　　　　　◇ dignity（n.）尊嚴
◇ counterattack（v.）反擊；反攻　　◇ suppress（v.）壓抑；克制

they had some bitter grudge against men, especially boys—as soon as those miscreants came around, the birds would attack for sure. The strangest thing was that they would always sing a lovely song before attacking.

There were some boys who, refusing to admit defeat, would counterattack by picking up rocks from the ground and throwing them at the birds. Once a bird goaded me into fighting back. A group of students passed by just then and, judging by their finger-pointing, got a big kick out of seeing an old man who was childish enough to throw rocks at birds. At the time, I was the greatest professor in the world; in order to maintain my professorial dignity, I was forced to suppress my ire and let the drongo attack without retaliating.

6-10

After that, every year in June, the black drongos would launch an assault on pedestrians (mostly the male ones). Why they chose that particular time remains a mystery. On one occasion, I was showing an important official around the campus. Officials like him are venerable, stately creatures, very dignified. The obstinate drongos, however, gave him no respect—they set their sights on him and swooped down. Caught off guard, the great official ducked down in fright. Now, you must know that such important people simply can't lose possession of themselves like that. Although all of us pretended

◇ retaliate (v.) 報復；報仇
◇ launch (v.) 展開
◇ assault (n.) 攻擊
◇ mystery (n.) 謎；難解之事
◇ official [əˋfɪʃəl] (n.) 官員
◇ venerable (adj.) 令人肅然起敬的

◇ dignified (adj.) 有威嚴的
◇ obstinate (adj.) 固執的；頑劣的
◇ duck (v.) 彎腰躲閃；低身逃避
◇ fright (n.) 害怕；畏懼
◇ pretend (v.) 假裝

　　因此我每次陪大官出巡，都希望能遇到烏秋來攻擊，可惜這件事再也沒有發生過。大概烏秋也知道，如果得罪了大官，清華的經費會被斬，清華經費少了，清華園裡的烏秋恐怕也活不下去了。

　　到了靜宜以後，雖然看到各種鳥，就是沒有看到過烏秋。

　　前些日子，我在清華的百齡堂開會，發現一位男孩在拿石頭打烏秋，才想到又是六月了。可愛的烏秋每年這時一定要攻擊男生，今年顯然仍不例外。在百齡堂可以聽到牠們可愛的攻擊前奏曲。

11　　我走了出去，烏秋對我看了一眼，無動於衷。一位傻呼呼的男學生走過，烏秋立刻對他俯衝下去，我這下才想起，烏秋也不攻擊老人的。

◇ incident（n.）事件
◇ inspection（n.）檢查；巡視
◇ budget（n.）預算
◇ survive（v.）存活；倖存
◇ Providence University 靜宜大學
◇ attend（v.）參加；出席

we hadn't seen, he had already lost a huge amount of face—we didn't really have to respect him after that.

After that incident, every time I went on campus inspection tours with important officials, I hoped we would be attacked by black drongos. Unfortunately, however, such a thing never happened again. It was probably because the drongos knew that if they offended an important official, Tsing Hua's budget would be cut, and if that happened, they would no longer be able to survive on the campus.

After I moved to Providence University, even though I saw all kinds of birds, I never saw black drongos.

A few days ago, I attended a meeting at Tsing Hua's Bailing Hall, where I found a boy throwing rocks at black drongos. That made me realize it was June again. The lovable drongos would always attack boys at this time of year, and this year was no exception. From within Bailing Hall, I could hear them singing the beautiful preludes to their attacks.

I walked outside, and a drongo looked at me without moving a muscle. Then a foolish, unsuspecting male student walked by, and the drongo immediately swooped down at him. It was then it occurred to me: black drongos don't attack old men.

11

◇ lovable(adj.)讓人疼愛的
◇ exception(n.)例外
◇ prelude(n.)序曲；前奏
◇ muscle(n.)肌肉

◇ unsuspecting(adj.)不疑有它的
◇ occur(v.)使(某人)想起(註：常用在 it occurs/ occurred to 某人)

(1) distinguish A from B 區分／辨別A與B（1段）

Its whole body is pitch black, and besides its smaller size, nothing about its appearance distinguishes it from a crow.

全身漆黑，除了體形比烏鴉小以外，其餘都像烏鴉。

解析

句子後半段 nothing about its appearance distinguishes it from a crow 比較難懂。讀者可以耐著性子，先從 distinguishes it from a crow 這個部分入手，意思為「令牠和烏鴉有所分別」。接著再看（nothing about its appearance），意思為「牠的外表沒有一處」，所以整個說來就是「牠的外表沒有一處令牠和烏鴉有所分別」，言下之意就是「牠和烏鴉一個樣」。此外，讀者還可以學習到「漆黑」的英文為 pitch black，所以「血紅」、「雪白」、「天藍」各該如何用英文表現呢？（blood red, snow white, sky blue）

小試身手

1. 他一頭亮紅頭髮讓他有別於班上其他人。

   _____

---

(2) swoop down on... 對（某人）直撲而來（2段）

The bird perched in a tree in front of me, where it sang beautifully for a while, then abruptly swooped down on me again.

這隻鳥飛到我前面的一棵樹上，先是用非常好聽的聲音叫了一陣子，然後又對我俯衝下來。

解析

動詞 swoop 即指由高處向低處快速俯衝而下，讀者不妨想像蒼鷹在天空盤旋，在發現獵物時，飛撲而下的那種畫面，就是 swoop down，如果地面

有隻不幸的兔子，成了蒼鷹的目標，那整個情節就是 The eagle swooped down on the poor rabbit.

小試身手

2. 那老鷹俯衝而下，伸出爪子，然後在空中攫住鴿子。

_____

(3) **lock onto...** 鎖定（目標）（2段）
　　look pleased with... 看起來很得意

It locked onto me like a target; then, as it reached my head, it pulled up and flew away, looking very pleased with itself.
牠以我為目標，到達我頭上以後，又拉起鳥頭，揚長而去。

解析

飛行員駕著戰鬥機，用雷達「鎖定」（lock onto）敵機，拇指按下按鈕，飛彈勁射而出，數秒之後敵機化作一團火球──原來清華校園出現過類似的空戰場面──烏秋「鎖定住」李教授，展開攻擊。看來李教授不是對手，否則怎麼小小鳥兒在「拉起機身」（pulled up）、「脫離空戰區」（flew away）後，會「一副自鳴得意的神情」（looking very pleased with itself）呢？作者描寫人鳥大戰，譯者也用了一些空戰術語來翻譯，讀者應該看得很過癮才是。

小試身手

3. 他給作品添上最後一筆，放下（畫）筆，一副很得意／滿意的樣子。

_____

（4）take it upon oneself to V 以……為己任（4段）

About two weeks later, a few black drongos took it upon themselves to dive at pedestrians along the main thoroughfares of the Tsing Hua campus.

大約有兩個星期左右，幾隻烏秋鳥專門在清華園的交通要道對行人俯衝攻擊。

解析

看到 take it upon oneself 這個片語，讀者可否隱約有幾分「以……為己任」的感受？用這個片語來詮釋原文裡的「專門……」也算一絕，非常詼諧。

小試身手

4. 他一直以保持社區清淨為己任。

_____

（5）to one's extreme displeasure 令某人非常之生氣；令某人氣得不得了（4段）

There were even a couple people who got scratched by the birds' claws, to their extreme displeasure.

有一兩位甚至被鳥爪抓到，氣得半死。

解析

「to one's +（情緒）」是個常見又重要的用法，相當於我們日常言談中「令（人）如何如何」之意，比如：

◈ 他沒搭那班在印尼墜毀的航機，令我放下心來。
To my great relief, he was not on the flight that crashed in Indonesia.

小試身手

5. 令我難過的是，他似乎不願意承認他的錯。

_____

---

(6) **have（a）grudge against...** 和……有仇／有恩怨／有過節（5段）

It was as though they had some bitter grudge against men, especially boys—as soon as those miscreants came around, the birds would attack for sure.

牠們似乎最恨男孩子，尤其是小男孩，這些頑童一來，牠們一定來攻擊。

解析

整個片語的核心字眼為 grudge，它本身的意思為「惡意」、「怨恨」或「不良的居心」。要表示「對某人懷有怨氣」，一般就是使用 have（a）grudge against someone，動詞的部分，除了這裡英譯的 have，使用 hold 也頗常見。

小試身手

6. 如果你對那些曾得罪你的人懷恨，你只會傷害自己。

_____

（7）**get a big kick out of Ving（or N）**看到……而大樂**（6段）**

A group of students passed by just then and, judging by their finger-pointing, got a big kick out of seeing an old man who was childish enough to throw rocks at birds.

路過的一群學生，看到我返老還童，用石頭打鳥，認為極為有趣，對我指指點點。

解析

欲學會這個片語，就要對 kick 有一番認識，讀者當然學習過此字，也知道它的意思為「踢」，但是請跳脫出來，從另一個面向來看這個字，它在此片語中為名詞，更重要的是，它是個俚俗的用法，指的是一種「在精神上或情緒上讓人為之一振或讓人為之興奮的感覺」、「刺激」。讀者們試想：半百年紀的老師學作小兒，撿石塊打鳥，學徒門生見之而大樂，這裡的 a big kick 即「大樂」是也。

小試身手

7. 我們看到了狗咬破了汽車的輪胎，都覺得有趣。

_____

（8）**be forced to V**被逼得……；不得不……**（6段）**

At the time, I was the greatest professor in the world; in order to maintain my professorial dignity, I was forced to suppress my ire and let the drongo attack without retaliating.

我當時已是世界上最偉大的教授，為了保持大教授的尊嚴，只好忍氣吞聲，讓烏秋攻擊而不還手。

解析

force 在此為動詞，為「強迫」、「逼迫」的意思，以被動語態 (be forced) 表現，就具備「被逼得……」或「不得不……」之意，說明一種非我所願，但是形勢比人強，不得不低頭的情況。be forced 之後常隨著不定詞 (to V)，以表示被逼得只好做某事。

小試身手

8. 村民們逼不得已棄農業改行挖礦。

_____

(9) launch an assault on... 對……發動攻擊(7段)

After that, every year in June, the black drongos would launch an assault on pedestrians (mostly the male ones).

以後每年六月，烏秋就會對行人(多半是男人)展開攻擊。

解析

「發射」太空船，英文為 launch a spacecraft；「展開」一個社會運動，英文為 launch a social movement。由此可見，動詞 launch 具有「發射」或「展開」的意思。片語 launch an assault on 自然就是「對……發動攻擊」。有時候可以用 attack 取代 assault，如以下的小試身手。

小試身手

9. 他們已擬好計畫要對政敵發動一連串的無情攻勢。

_____

(10) remain a mystery 依然成謎（7段）

Why they chose that particular time remains a mystery.

為什麼選這個時間，至今是個謎。

【解析】

「依／仍然……」無論中英文的言談場合都常會使用到，中文說「依然是個秘密」、「依然如故」、「仍然無解」以英文表示分別為 remain a secret/ remain unchanged/ remain unsolved。

以下這句英文使用到 remain，你認為是什麼意思呢？

◇For people in certain areas of the world, democracy remains as remote as the stars in the sky.

小試身手

10. 在某些回教國家，在公開場所和女人說話仍然是禁忌。

_____

---

(11) set one's sights on 瞄準……；對準……（7段）

The obstinate drongos, however, gave him no respect—they set their sights on him and swooped down.

偏偏烏秋不識相，對準了他俯衝而來。

【解析】

讀者只要記住，片語裡的名詞 sight 指的是槍管上方用以瞄準目標的「準星」、「瞄準器」，那麼整個片語的意義就迎刃而解：「將準星對著……」當然，大部分時候這個片語已經脫離殺伐的戰場，引申到其他領域，比如：

◇ Now he has set his sights on a more meaningful career.

（12）（be）caught off guard 疏於防備（7段）

Caught off guard, the great official ducked down in fright.
大官一慌之下，蹲了下去。

解析

非常好的片語，一定要學起來。guard 在此處為名詞，是「防衛、防備」之意。人在心理或生理上都有「自我防衛機制」來應付一些突如其來的狀況，但百密終有一疏，謹慎戒懼之心稍有鬆懈（off guard），常常就會「中伏受擊（get/ be caught）」。因此，(be)caught off guard 即用以表示此種「情急之下」的狀況。

（13）lose possession of oneself 失態（7段）

Now, you must know that such important people simply can't lose possession of themselves like that.
需知大人物是不可以如此失態的。

解析

欲學習 lose possession of oneself 這個片語不妨從 possession of oneself

下手，而欲學習 possession of oneself 又可以從 self-possessed 這個字入門。此字的意思為「鎮定自持；沉著自若」，因此 possession of oneself 也是「鎮定自持；沉著自若」，如果之前再添加動詞 lose，就是「慌張失態」的意思。

小試身手

13. 在那種危急的情況，大多數人都會慌張失態。

_____

(14) lose a huge amount of face 顏面盡失；丟臉到家 (7段)

Although all of us pretended we hadn't seen, he had already lost a huge amount of face—we didn't really have to respect him after that.
雖然我們大家全體假裝沒有看見，他已是大丟其臉，我們以後再也不必太尊敬他了。

解析

何謂「面子」？「尊嚴」是也。愛面子的心理人皆有之，中國人似乎特別嚴重。中文和英文都選擇「臉」(face) 來詮釋這種潛伏於人心幽微之處的「面子或尊嚴」(face/ dignity)。「厚臉皮」、「不要臉」、「死要面子」、「拉不下臉來」都是和「面子」有關的習語。英文方面，則有 lose face 和 save face (注意：不是 save one's face) 等用語。「一心想扳回失去的面子常常更失面子」，裡子應該比面子更重要。

小試身手

14. 如果有需要，他會想盡辦法來挽回顏面。

_____

(15)（be）no exception 自不例外（10段）

The lovable drongos would always attack boys at this time of year, and this year was no exception.

可愛的烏秋每年這時一定要攻擊男生，今年顯然仍不例外。

解析

很重要，同時也是很好學的一個用語。名詞 exception 本身即為「例外」的意思，因此 (be)no exception 自然就是「自不例外」，可以指事，亦可指人。

小試身手

15. 每個人都被數學老師處罰，即使最得老師歡心（teacher's pet）的 Jolin 也不例外。

_____

(16) without moving a muscle 文風不動；動也不動（11段）

I walked outside, and a drongo looked at me without moving a muscle.

我走了出去，烏秋對我看了一眼，無動於衷。

解析

不經意地眨眨眼睛，順順頭髮，口渴了拿杯水喝，看到朋友打招呼問好，這些簡單的動作在生物學家和物理學家看來卻是很複雜的肌肉運動。以人體來說，一舉手，一抬足，可能不是 move a muscle 就做得出來的，Any movement requires a concerted effort of many muscles. 說了這麼多，到底什麼是 muscle？就是動物身上的「肌肉」，動物能「動」，其實就是肌肉牽動的結果，所以 moving a muscle 就是「動」的意思，前面安置介詞 without，動詞由 move 變為動名詞 moving，而整個的意思為「動也不動」、「不動聲色」。

小試身手

16. 千萬別動！有人來了。

_____

（17）it occurs/ occurred to someone 某人忽焉想到某事（11段）

It was then it occurred to me: black drongos don't attack old men.

我這下才想起，烏秋也不攻擊老人的。

解析

這是個非常固定的句型。以下來做個練習：

◇ 我爸爸媽媽忽然想到家裡的爐子沒關掉。

對初學者而言，要成功表達這個句子充滿了危機，也許字詞片語都會：「我爸爸媽媽」為 my parents；「家裡的爐子」為 the stove in the house；「沒關掉」為 forgot to turn off。可是要寫出整句的：「我爸爸媽媽忽然想到家裡的爐子沒關掉。」得如何著手呢？讀者們在把這個句型融會貫通後，你就知道要這麼做：

It suddenly occurred to my parents that they'd forgotten to turn off the stove in the house.

小試身手

17. 我一生中從沒想到會有機會成為總統候選人。

_____

小試身手解答

1.　His bright red hair distinguishes him from his classmates.

2.　The hawk swooped down, stretched out its claws and snatched the dove in midair.

3.　He gave the work a finishing touch and put down his brush, looking very pleased with himself.

4.　He's always taken it upon himself to keep the community clean.

5.　Much to my regret, he didn't seem to want to acknowledge his mistake.

6.　You'll only hurt yourself by holding grudges against those who have offended you. 或 If you hold grudges against those who have offended you, you'll only hurt yourself.

7.　We all got a kick out of seeing the dog chew a hole in the car tire.

8.　The villagers were forced to give up agriculture for mining.

9.　They have set up a plan to launch a series of relentless attacks on their political enemies.

10.　In certain Muslim countries, talking to a woman in a public place remains a taboo.

11.　"There are so many beautiful ladies here," he joked. "Have you set your sights on any of them?"

12. His question caught me off guard. I opened my mouth, but no answer came out.

13. Most people would lose possession of themselves in a crisis like that.

14. He would do anything necessary to save face.

15. Everyone was punished by our math teacher. Even Jolin, the teacher's pet, was no exception.

16. Don't move a muscle! Someone's coming.

17. All my life it never occurred to me（或 Never in my life did it occur to me）that I would have the chance of becoming a presidential candidate.

Side Effects

副作用

1-5　　作為一位心理學教授，難免會有人要來找你，卻又不肯到醫院去看病的情形。這種人往往都是社會上的知名人士，他們心理上如有問題，當然不願意讓別人知道，這時，他們就會悄悄地來找我這種人了。

　　這次來的人是社會上家喻戶曉的工業家，當年從我們學校畢業的時候，就以有領導能力出了名，不到幾年，他的事業就扶搖直上。一般人對他的評價是他特別冷靜，從不慌亂，判斷力更是相當正確，他的成功，一直是坊間書籍津津樂道的對象。誰都羨慕他，中小學生都暗暗地希望能像他這樣，白手起家，建立一個龐大的工業王國。

　　這位名人進來的時候，卻流露出一種非常嚴重的焦慮心情，他直截了當地說：「我想自殺」。對我而言，這當然是想像不到的，這位被人人羨慕的社會知名人物，為什麼如此沮喪呢？

　　他告訴我他之所以想自殺，是因為他有一個毛病，他無法「愛人」。我還是第一次聽到這種怪病，這個年頭，大多數的人都會埋怨

CD2-5
◇ psychology [saɪˋkɑləʒɪ] (n.) 心理學
◇ inevitably (adv.) 避免不了地
◇ celebrity [səˋlɛbrətɪ] (n.) 名人
◇ industrial tycoon [taɪˋkun] 企業鉅子；

企業大亨
◇ household name 家喻戶曉的人物
◇ renowned (adj.) 著名的
◇ leadership ability 領導能力

If you're a psychology professor, there will inevitably be people
who want to visit with you but are unwilling to go to a hospital to
do so. These people are often celebrities; if they have psychological
problems, they naturally want to keep them secret. That's when
they'll quietly come looking for someone like me.

1-5
CD2-3

On this particular occasion, the man who came to see me was
an industrial tycoon, a household name. Back when he graduated
from our school, he was already renowned for his leadership ability;
in a few short years, his career took off like a rocket. The average
person's assessment of him was that he was exceptionally calm and
collected: he never panicked, and he possessed remarkably accurate
powers of judgment. Authors never tired of writing about his success
in their books. Everyone envied him, and even elementary and
middle school students secretly wished they could do what he had
done: build a vast industrial empire out of virtually nothing.

But as this celebrity walked in, he betrayed a very severe anxiety.
He got straight to the point: "I want to kill myself." To me, of course,
this was unimaginable. Why did this man, a social icon and the object
of universal envy, feel so depressed?

He told me the reason he wanted to kill himself was that he had a
flaw: he was unable to "love others". This was the first time I had

---

◇ assessment (n.) 評價；評鑑
◇ panic (v.) 恐慌
◇ possess (v.) 擁有；持有
◇ powers of judgment 判斷力
◇ industrial empire 企業王國

◇ betray (v.) 流露；顯露
◇ unimaginable (adj.) 難以想像的
◇ social icon ['aɪkɑn] 社會偶像人物
◇ depressed (adj.) 沮喪；情緒低落

沒有人愛,感到社會的冷漠。自己承認無法愛人,一心在想自殺,這還是我第一次碰到。

於是他告訴我他的奇遇。

6-10　　在他大四的時候,他已是同學中企圖心非常強的一位,有一天,學校裡心理系的一位名教授把他叫去,問他肯不肯參與一個秘密的實驗。這位名教授可以給他一種發明的藥,吃了藥以後,他的判斷力會更好,人也會更加冷靜,觀察力會相當敏銳,以他現在既有的學問,加上這些特別的能力,將來一定可以事業成功,在社會上扶搖直上。

他雖然對這種藥有興趣,可是他也知道任何藥都會有副作用的,所以他立刻問那位教授這種藥有沒有副作用,教授告訴他,他只要吃五顆就夠了,在生理上副作用幾乎沒有,可是這種藥卻有一種奇怪的副作用,吃了藥以後,就會喪失了愛人的能力。

◇ ailment(n.)疾病
◇ recognize(v.)認知;體認
◇ ambitious(adj.)雄心壯志的;有抱負理想的
◇ participate(in)(v.)參加;參與
◇ pressure(n.)壓力
◇ powers of observation 觀察力

heard of such a strange ailment. In this day and age, the vast majority of people complain about how no one in this cold society loves them. Never before had I met a man who was bent on killing himself because he recognized his inability to love others.

Then he told me his remarkable story.

When he was a senior in college, he was already one of the most ambitious members of his class. One day, a renowned professor from the psychology department called him into his office to ask if he'd be willing to participate in a secret experiment. The professor said he could give him a type of drug he had invented. If he took the drug, his analytical ability would improve, he'd stay cooler under pressure and his powers of observation would sharpen. Given the level of education he had already attained and the special abilities the drug would give him, his career would be sure to succeed, and he would quickly rise to prominence.

6-10

Although he was very interested in the drug, he also knew that all drugs have side effects, so he immediately asked the professor if this particular drug had any. The professor said that all he'd have to do was take five pills. There would be virtually no physiological side effects, but the drug would cause an unusual side effect: taking it would render him unable to love others.

◇ sharpen (v.) 變得敏銳
◇ level of education 教育程度
◇ prominence (n.) 傑出；卓越

◇ side effects 副作用
◇ physiological [ˌfɪzɪəˈlɑdʒɪkl̩] (adj.) 生理的

我的病人對於無法愛人，不太在乎，他認為這好像沒有什麼關係。他問教授會不會仍有被愛的能力，教授說他仍會感到別人對他的愛，只是不能愛人而已。

他覺得似乎值得一試，因為他知道在社會上所有成功的人不僅因為他們工作得非常努力，最重要的是他們的觀察力特別敏銳，判斷力也特別正確。他當時一心一意要在社會上出人頭地，雖然吃了藥以後，不能愛人，反正仍能感到被愛，因此他答應了。

教授卻非常小心，一再問他對藥的副作用了解了沒有，他說他了解，而且也願意冒這個險，於是教授給了他五顆藥，他照指示在五天內吃了這五顆藥。

11-15 藥性果真很靈，他進入社會以後，大家都稱讚他的觀察力和判斷力，他的決定十有八九都是對的，難怪他的事業蒸蒸日上，誰也比不上他。

◇ overly（adv.）**過度地；非常地**
◇ sharp-eyed（adj.）**眼光銳利的；眼尖的**
◇ adept（adj.）**熟練的；專精的**
◇ cautious（adj.）**謹慎的；小心的**

My patient wasn't overly concerned about not being able to love others, as he thought it wouldn't present much of a problem for him. He asked the professor whether he would still be able to be loved. The professor said he would still feel the love that others had for him—he just wouldn't be able to love them back.

He felt like it was worth a try, for he knew that all successful people in society had achieved what they had not merely by being very hard workers, but more importantly by being particularly sharp-eyed observers and adept analyzers. At that time, his heart was absolutely set on making a name for himself in society. Although he'd be unable to love others if he took the drug, at any rate he'd still feel loved. So he agreed to do the experiment.

The professor, however, was very cautious; he repeatedly asked my patient whether he fully understood the side effect of the drug. My patient said he did, and he was willing to take the risk. And so the professor gave him the five pills, which he swallowed within five days as instructed.

Sure enough, the drug worked. When he started working, everyone **11-15** praised his keen eye and sharp intuition. The vast majority of his decisions were good ones. It was hardly surprising that his career improved by leaps and bounds—no one could compare with him.

◇ as instructed 依照指示　　　　　◇ intuition [ˌɪntjuˈɪʃən] (n.) 直覺

　　可是他終於發現藥的副作用非常可怕，因為他變成了一個十分冷漠的人，他從不同情任何人，也對任何人都沒有什麼感情，即使他的母親去世，眼見他的弟弟哀痛欲絕，他卻什麼感覺都沒有，他的太太和孩子都知道他對他們毫無感情可言，他的部下更加感到他是世界上最冷漠的人。

　　他開始發現他失去了世界上最大的快樂，他的理智告訴他，付出比得到更有意義，他冷眼觀察社會上真正快樂的人都是對別人充滿愛心的人，這些人事業都比不上他，可是只因為他們能夠關懷別人，內心充滿平安的他們快樂多了。他雖然很希望也能如此，可一直做不到，大概藥性太強了。

　　他雖然號稱可以感受到別人的愛，可是因為他不愛人，也沒有什麼人愛他。最糟糕的是，給他藥的教授已去世了，他無法去問他要解藥。他知道我是這位名教授的親傳弟子，也已是大牌教授，所以他只好來找我，希望我替他弄到解藥。

◇ horrific（adj.）可怕的
◇ transform（v.）改變
◇ indifferent（adj.）冷漠的；沒有感情的
◇ devastated（adj.）悲不自勝的；哀慟的

Eventually, though, he discovered just how horrific the drug's side effect was: it transformed him into a cold, indifferent person. He never felt empathy or warmth for anyone. Even when his mother passed away, he could plainly see that his brother was devastated, but he felt nothing at all. His wife and kids knew all too well that he had no real affection for them, and his underlings felt sure that he was the world's most coldhearted man.

He began to realize he had lost the greatest happiness on earth. His intellect told him that it was more meaningful to give than to receive. With cold detachment, he saw how the happiest people in society were those who were full of love for others. Career-wise, they couldn't measure up to him, but because they were able to feel compassion, their hearts were filled with peace, and they were much happier than he was. Although he wished he could be like them, he simply couldn't—it seemed the drug was just too powerful.

Although he was supposedly still able to feel others' love for him, because he didn't love anybody, nobody really loved him. The worst thing was that the professor who gave him the drug had passed away, so he couldn't ask him for an antidote. He knew, however, that the professor had passed much of his knowledge down to me and that I was already a renowned professor in my own right, so he figured the next best thing to do was to come and see if I could find an antidote for him instead.

◇ underling (n.) 下屬；部下
◇ coldhearted (adj.) 冷酷無情的
◇ intellect (n.) 才智；理智
◇ detachment (n.) 疏離；超脫
◇ compassion (n.) 同情；愛心
◇ antidote (n.) 解藥

　　我覺得這件事實在古怪之至，因為我從未聽過這種藥，我本來想立刻拒絕他的，可是看他不斷地要求，只好答應他試試看。我利用電腦作了大規模的文獻搜尋，發現從未有人提過這種藥，據我記憶所及，這位名教授也從未向我提起這一個秘密的實驗，我更沒有聽過人的愛心是可以受藥物控制的。

16-20　　虧得我想起一件事，這位名教授去世以後，校方為了表示對他的尊重，曾經請他的遺孀捐出所有他的工作日誌，我因此請圖書館讓我進入保存他日誌的特別房間。我發現他的日誌是以日期排列的，我算一算那位病人在本校畢業的年份，一頁一頁地看，果然被我找到這個秘密實驗的詳細紀錄。

　　對我而言，這個實驗實在太有意義了，我看了紀錄以後，也做出了解藥。

　　病人來了，我告訴他我已弄清楚這是怎麼一回事，因此我已對症下藥，吃了我的藥以後，他可以恢復人類愛人的本能，可是這種藥也有

◇ bizarre [bɪˋzɑr] (adj.) 怪異的；詭譎的
◇ persist (in) (v.) 繼續不斷
◇ thorough [ˋθɝo] (adj.) 徹底的；完整的
◇ gesture (n.) 手勢；表示
◇ widow (n.) 寡婦
◇ chronologically (adv.) 依時間先後順序的
◇ calculate (v.) 計算
◇ thumb (through) (v.) 翻閱

I thought this whole thing was truly bizarre—I had never heard of such a drug in my life. At first I was tempted to turn him away then and there, but seeing how he persisted in pleading for help, I had to promise that I'd try. I did a thorough search on my computer, but I found that no one had ever mentioned a drug like that. As far as I could recall, the professor had never mentioned this secret experiment to me, and I had certainly never heard that human love could be controlled by a drug.

Fortunately, I remembered something: after the professor passed away, as a gesture of respect, the university had asked his widow to donate all his work logs to them. Therefore, I asked the librarian to let me into the special room where his logs were kept. I found that they were ordered chronologically. After calculating the date the patient had graduated, I thumbed through page by page until, sure enough, I found a detailed record of the secret experiment.

I found the experiment absolutely fascinating. After looking over the record, I concocted an antidote.

When my patient came again, I told him that I had figured the whole thing out and prescribed a drug to solve his problem. If he decided to take my pills, his ability to love others would be restored, but this drug, too, would have side effects: after taking it, his analytical ability might not be as reliable as before, and his powers of

◇ detailed (adj.) 詳細的；詳盡的
◇ fascinating (adj.) 令人著迷的；令人動心的
◇ concoct [kən`kɑkt] (v.) 調製
◇ prescribe (v.) 開（藥）
◇ restore (v.) 恢復
◇ reliable [rɪ`laɪəb!] (adj.) 可靠的

副作用,吃藥以後判斷力可能不像過去那樣正確,觀察力也可能不再敏銳。如果他的事業因此走下坡,可不能怪我。

我的病人對他的事業毫不在乎,他只想能夠充滿愛人與享受愛人的樂趣。

我一再問他是否真的想要無私地愛人,他一再回答他的確如此,因此我用一只小瓶子裝了這五顆藥給他,他謝謝我,匆匆地走了。

21-25 　　三個月以後,病人回來了,他這次變了一個人。他說他已經感受到關懷別人所帶來的心靈上的平安,他告訴我他發現他的一位下屬的太太得了癌症,過去他對這種消息會完全無動於衷,這一次他主動地表示關心,雖然她仍去世了。可是他卻從頭到尾分擔大家的痛苦,也使他對死亡有深一層的了解。

　　他的另一位下屬有一個兒子在念國中,這位下屬收入不多,無法讓兒子請最好的家教,他主動表示願意幫這位國中生的忙,這位國中生的考試成績,果真大為進步,使他高興極了。

◇ delight (n.) 歡喜;快樂;樂趣
◇ unselfishly (adj.) 無私地
◇ emphatic [ɪmˋfætɪk] (adj.) 加重語氣的
◇ totally (adv.) 完全地;全然地

observation might lose some of their sharpness. If his career were to go downhill as a result, he had better not blame me.

My patient didn't care about his career in the least—he only wanted to be filled with love again, to enjoy the delight of loving.

Repeatedly I asked if he really wanted to unselfishly love others, and repeatedly he answered with an emphatic "yes". And so I put the five pills into a small bottle and gave it to him. He thanked me and hurried away.

Three months later, my patient returned, this time as a totally different person. He said he had felt the inner peace that comes from caring for others. He told me he'd found out that the wife of one of his subordinates had cancer. Before, he would have been completely unmoved by such news; this time, however, he actively expressed concern, even though she eventually passed away. But he shared the family's pain throughout their ordeal, and he gained a deeper understanding of death.

21-25

Another of his workers had a son in middle school, but his salary was too low for him to hire a good tutor for the boy. Without being asked, my patient said he'd be willing to help the boy, and he was overjoyed to see his test scores go way up as a result.

◇ subordinate (n.) 屬下；部屬
◇ unmoved (adj.) 無動於衷的
◇ actively (adv.) 主動地；積極地

◇ tutor (n.) 家教；私人教師
◇ test scores 考試成績（分數）

　　至於他的事業，他說他的事業似乎仍然不受影響。

　　我的病人謝了我以後，最後還是問了我一個最不願意回答的問題，究竟這是什麼藥？為什麼從來沒有人談過藥物可以左右人的愛心？

　　我只好告訴他，我其實給了他維他命而已。當年，那位名教授也是給了他維他命。他的工作日誌上寫得一清二楚。人是有自由意志的；行善或行惡，都是人自己的事。你如立志做好人，就可以成為好人，你如冷酷無情，實在不該怪別人，我的病人年輕時，就只想成功，即使不能愛人，也在所不惜。那位名教授只是成全了他的志願而已。這次他已下定決心要愛人，我也只是給了他心理上的維他命而已。

26-30　　我們都知道希特勒做了很多壞事，可是沒有聽說他是在某一種藥物控制之下做的，我們更知道，既然在希特勒屠殺猶太人的時候，很多德國人犧牲自己的生命來拯救猶太人，這些人也從未在藥物的控制之下。

　　人是有自由意志的，我們也許不能控制自己的命運，可是只要下

◇ manipulate [mə`nɪpjəˌlet] (v.) 操控；控制　　◇ unfeeling (adj.) 沒有感情的
◇ originally (adv.) 原本地　　◇ grant (v.) 應允；答應給
◇ bear (v.) 承擔；擔當　　◇ determine (v.) 決定
◇ resolve (v.) 決意要；下決心要

As for his career, he said it didn't seem to have been impacted yet.

After thanking me, my patient finally asked me the question that I really didn't want to answer: just what drug was this anyway? Why had no one ever mentioned that a drug could manipulate human love?

I was forced to admit that the pills I had given him were really nothing more than vitamins. The drug the famous professor originally gave him was also just vitamins, as his work log clearly recorded. Man is a creature of free will; each person bears sole responsibility for the good or evil he chooses to do. If you resolve to be a good person, you can become one; if you're cold and unfeeling, you ought not to blame others. When my patient was young, the only thing he wanted was success, even if it came at the cost of losing the ability to love. The professor had merely granted his own wish. Now, he himself had determined to love others—all I had done was give him a few psychological vitamins.

We all know Hitler did all kinds of bad things, but never once have we heard he did them because he was controlled by a drug. We know equally well that when Hitler was massacring Jews, many Germans sacrificed their lives to save them, likewise without ever being controlled by a drug. 26-30

No man is bereft of free will. Perhaps we cannot control our

◇ Hitler 希特勒（將德國帶向第二次世界大戰的罪魁禍首）
◇ massacre ['mæsəkɚ] (v.) 屠殺
◇ Jew (n.) 猶太人
◇ German (n.) 德國人
◇ sacrifice (v.) 犧牲
◇ bereft (adj.) 失去（常用於片語 be bereft of）

定決心，是可以控制自己的行為的，我們都應該為我們的所作所為負責。

病人輕鬆地謝謝我，他說他有一件禮物要給我，我打開了禮物，發現這是我給他的五顆維他命，換了一個更漂亮的瓶子裝。他顯然一顆也沒有吃。

我窘得不得了，聰明還被聰明誤，這次我被他騙了。

病人告訴我，這次他非常小心。他將藥帶到一位藥學系的教授那裡去，那位教授一眼就看出這是最廉價的維他命。

31-33　病人是個有智慧的人，他終於想通了，過去他是自己企圖心的奴隸，如果他將自己從他的強烈企圖心解放出來，他一生會恢復自由的。

世界上很少人知道，人最大的快樂來自給予，而不來自得到。我的這位病人是個聰明人，他雖然很晚才悟到這個道理，可是他倒是覺悟得特別的徹底。

◇ behavior（n.）行為
◇ seal（v.）密封
◇ outsmart（v.）聰明過人（此處 had outsmarted myself 近於中文「聰明反被聰明誤」之意）
◇ trick（v.）欺騙；瞞過（此處相當於中文「中計；中圈套」）

destinies, but as long as we firmly determine to do so, we can control our behavior. We should all take responsibility for our own actions.

After casually thanking me, the patient said he had a gift for me. When I opened the gift, I found that it was the five vitamin pills I had given him, now sealed in a nicer-looking bottle. Clearly he hadn't taken a single one.

I was at a loss for words. I had outsmarted myself—this time I was the one who had been tricked.

The patient told me that he was very cautious this time. He took the pills to a professor of pharmaceutics, who could tell at a glance that they were the most ordinary of vitamins.

The patient was a smart man; finally the answer came to him. 31-33
Hitherto, he had been the slave of his own ambition, but if he liberated himself from its powerful grip, his life would be free again.

Very few people in the world understand that man's greatest happiness comes from giving, not from receiving. This patient of mine was a wise man. Although it had taken him a long time to grasp this truth, he had grasped it especially well.

◇ pharmaceutics [ˌfɑrməˈsjutɪks] (n.) 藥學（研究製藥、配藥與藥性藥效的科學）
◇ slave (n.) 奴隸　　　　　　　◇ liberate (v.) 解脫；解放
◇ ambition (n.) 抱負；雄心　　　◇ grasp (v.) 懂；理解

　　我看到他的漂亮積架汽車停在樓下，上次來時有一位司機開車，這次他自己開車了，大概他知道司機晚上要休息的。

I saw his beautiful Jaguar parked below. Last time he came, he had had a chauffeur, but this time he drove himself. He must have known the driver would appreciate having the night off.

（1）keep something secret 不欲人知；嚴守秘密（1段）

...if they have psychological problems, they naturally want to keep them secret.

他們心理上如有問題，當然不願意讓別人知道。

解析

現代社會工作壓力巨大，人際關係緊繃，隨之而生的「心理問題」層出不窮，這心理問題，英文以 psychological problems 或 mental problems 表示，把某事（something）嚴守住（keep），使之成為一種秘密（secret），不為他人知道，當然表達起來就是 keep something secret 了。相反地，如果把某事公諸於世，一般就以 reveal something 或 expose something 等表示。

小試身手

1. 雖然那不算多麼私密（confidential）的事，但是我仍決意（determined）不讓他人知道。

   _____

（2）be renowned for... 以……出名（2段）

Back when he graduated from our school, he was already renowned for his leadership ability...

當年從我們學校畢業的時候，（他）就以有領導能力出了名……

解析

英文用字，相當於中文的「出名的」，就頗有幾個字，常見的除了這裡所見的 renowned，還有如下：famous, noted, well-known, celebrated, distinguished

等。這些字字義相近，所以用法也跟著很類似，比如，幾乎之後都可以接介詞 for 以表示「因……」而聞名、而享譽。

小試身手

2. 那位醫生因精湛的腦部手術技術而聞名。

_____

（3）the object of universal envy 人人稱羨的對象；舉世推崇的目標（3段）

Why did this man, a social icon and the object of universal envy, feel so depressed?

這位被人人羨慕的社會知名人物，為什麼如此沮喪呢？

解析

object 是「目標」、「對象」而 universal envy 則為「人人艷羨」的意思，所以 the object of universal envy 自然就是「眾人渴慕的目標」。一個人因為豐功偉業成了眾人目光的焦點，洞見觀瞻，應該壓力不小吧！若壓力無法得到適當紓解，可能沮喪憂鬱的症狀就出現了，這種身心狀態，英文名之為 depressed，名詞為 depression，是現代人的一大困擾。譯文裡另有 social icon 一詞，指的是「社會大眾的偶像人物」，是眾人仿效崇拜的典範。

小試身手

3. 她的新電影飽受批評。

_____

（4）be bent on... 一心一意想要……（4段）

Never before had I met a man who was bent on killing himself because he recognized his inability to love others.

自己承認無法愛人，一心在想自殺，這還是我第一次碰到。

解析

bent 是由動詞 bend 所衍生而來的形容詞，同時兼有兩種含意，一個和動詞原意較接近，當「彎曲」或「折彎」，另一個則是「決心的」、「心意已定的」。往深一層思考，其實兩個意思之間還是有關聯的。試想，當一個人的心意已決，就如一根撓曲變形的鐵棒，要把它扳直回來，恐怕就很費事了。所以，心意已定已決，難以改變轉變，很適合以這個片語表達。

小試身手

4. 她決心在三十歲前賺到第一個一百萬。

_____

（5） Given... 如果有……；假如……；考慮到……（6段）

Given the level of education he had already attained and the special abilities the drug would give him, his career would be sure to succeed, and he would quickly rise to prominence.

以他現在既有的學問，加上這些特別的能力，將來一定可以事業成功，在社會上扶搖直上。

解析

如果告訴你，這個 given 在這裡是個介詞的作用，你會嚇一大跳嗎？事實就是如此，英文就是有一類稀有的介詞如 considering, regarding, excepting, save, but 等，讀者應該也觀察到一個有趣的現象，其中好幾個字竟然都是現在分詞（Ving）的形態。為什麼說它們是介詞而不是現在分詞呢？主要的理

由是它們的後面都接有受詞，以本句來說，given 的後面就有個 the level of education he had already attained and the special abilities the drug would give him（這個受詞真的好長）當它的受詞。當然這個在形式上是個過去分詞（Ven 或 Vpp），但是在作用上絕對是介詞的功能，和現在分詞不同。現在分詞無論是當分詞或介詞，有可能後面跟著受詞，但是過去分詞不可能後面還跟著受詞的。不過，對學習英文的人來說，這裡最重要的事情是，這個 given 要作何種解釋？它表示的是一種「以……作為計算或推估的依據」的情況。所以原文 Given the level of education he had already attained and the special abilities the drug would give him... 的字面語意就是「以他已經具備的教育程度和這種藥物所賦予他的特殊能力來推估……」。

小試身手

5. 考量到他的愚鈍，他不會發財，除非他的運氣好。

_____

---

(6) ...rise to prominence 顯赫；揚名（6段）

例句同上

解析

prominence 一字表達「傑出」、「卓越」的意思。「傑出」和「卓越」都不是天生或一蹴而就的事，而是一步一腳印，逐步往上爬升，才有可能到所謂「頭角崢嶸」、「無人能出其右」的地位吧，而這個過程，用一個 rise（上升；爬升）來表示，如日月之由地平線升至天頂，不是傳神達意之至嗎？萬丈紅塵很多事情，可都要由低向高，步步攀升的，「成名」rise to fame 如是，「爬到有權力的地位」rise to power 不也如是？讀者只要立志持恆，英文能力要提升至精熟的程度 rise to a high level of proficiency 絕對是大大有可能的事情。

小試身手

6. 他年少成名。

_____

（7）...render someone unable to V... 令（某人）無法……（7段）

There would be virtually no physiological side effects, but the drug would cause an unusual side effect: taking it would render him unable to love others.

在生理上副作用幾乎沒有，可是這種藥卻有一種奇怪的副作用，吃了藥以後，就會喪失了愛人的能力。

解析

這個句型的關鍵詞是這個動詞 render，它的意思是「令（人）陷於某種狀態」，比如：

◇ 那種藥讓他亢奮睡不著：
The drug rendered him agitated and sleepless.

再者，巧婦難為無米之炊，若一個方案因為預算不足而難以為繼，我們想說「緊縮的預算使得這個計劃難以產生令人滿意的結果。」則英文表達如下：
Budget constraints rendered it impossible for the project to yield satisfactory results.

小試身手

7. 他的羞怯讓他無法和他人很自然暢快地（comfortably）來往交際（socialize）。

_____

(8) one's heart is set on... ; one has his heart set on...
（某人）一心一意要……（9段）

At that time, his heart was absolutely set on making a name for himself in society.

他當時一心一意要在社會上出人頭地。

解析

這個看似冗長的片語其實並不難學，因為很容易從字面就可以理解出它的含意，someone's heart is set on something「某人的心擺在某事上面」，不就等於說「某人一心想做某事」嗎？此片語的另一種形式 someone has his heart set on something 也常出現。

另外一個值得注意的地方是 make a name for oneself 這個片語，這也是個從字面就可以窺知意義的片語，「為自己締造名（氣）」，不就是中文常說的「顯名聲」、「揚名立萬」嗎？

小試身手

8-1. 她的父母希望她成為醫生，但她一心想做藝術方面的工作。

_____

8-2. 只有很小百分比的人能在這個世界上揚名立萬。

_____

---

(9) it is hardly surprising that... ……不足為奇（11段）

It was hardly surprising that his career improved by leaps and bounds—no one could compare with him.

難怪他的事業蒸蒸日上，誰也比不了他。

解析

surprising 是個大家都不陌生的字,具有「令人驚奇」、「令人意外」的意思。讀者對 surprising 之前的 hardly 可不能掉以輕心,它是個否定副詞,為「幾乎不」的意思,所以 hardly surprising 就成了「不感意外」、「沒什麼驚奇的」之意,再配合前面的虛主詞 it,就構成了本句型,用來表示「(某事)不足為奇」,而這個某事就置於 it is hardly surprising 之後的 that 子句表達之。

小試身手

9. 照我們冷氣機的使用量來看,電費會這麼高也沒什麼好驚訝的。

　　　　　　　　　　　　　　　　　　　　　　　　　　

(10) by leaps and bounds(尤其指進度,進展)快速地;神速地 (10段)

例句同上一句型

解析

進步有牛步式的進步,也有飛躍式,彈跳式的進步。bound 和 leap 這兩個名詞都是「大跳」的意思,所以,當某人學習做某事「突飛猛進」,就很適合以 improve by leaps and bounds 這個片語表示。

小試身手

10. 剛開始她跑得並不快,但不久她就有很大的進步。

(11) transform someone into... 把（某人）轉變成……（12段）

Eventually, though, he discovered just how horrific the drug's side effect was: it transformed him into a cold, indifferent person.

可是他終於發現藥的副作用非常可怕，因為他變成了一個十分冷漠的人。

解析

或許我們可以來做個拆字遊戲，把 transform 這個字拆成 trans- 和 form 兩部分。trans- 表示「改變」、「轉變」，而 form 則表示「外表」、「形體」。所以 transform 就造成了「變形」的意思，後面接個受詞，再接介詞 into 來表示「成為」，三個字的組合，構成了「把某人轉化成為……」的基本意涵。讀者們，看過電影史瑞克吧？影片中女主角被施了法術，長相變得和嗚嗝鬼（ogre）一樣令人望之卻步，（對不起，「嗚嗝鬼」是我自己的音譯，他就是男主角史瑞克，相貌讓你看了直想嗝。）但是，愛感動了一切，愛改變了一切……

小試身手

11. 魔棒（magic wand）輕輕一碰，那個嗚嗝鬼（ogre）就被變回一位美貌的公主。

＿＿＿＿＿＿＿＿＿＿＿＿＿＿＿＿＿＿＿＿＿＿＿＿＿＿＿＿

(12) can't measure up to someone 難以企及；難望某人項背（12段）

Career-wise, they couldn't measure up to him, but...

這些人事業都比不上他，可是……

解析

動詞 measure 的本意為「測量」、「衡量」，加上副詞 up 和介詞 to，就產生

了「符合某種標準」或「達到某種程度」的意思。有些父母親望子女成龍成鳳之心太過急切，常帶給子女莫大的心理壓力。這些子女們心理常生出一種感覺，不是他們不努力，而是父母的標準太苛太高，根本難以達到。這樣的孩子也許在心裡感嘆說："However hard I try, I can never measure up to their expectations."（無論怎麼努力，我就是達不到父母的期許）。

例句中另一個值得一提的地方是 career-wise 這個字裡的 -wise，就相當於中文的「在……方面」或「就……而言」。所以，你想說：「我的朋友 Smart 在智力方面是班上最出色的。」英文可得這麼說：

Intelligence-wise, my friend Smart is the most outstanding in the class.

小試身手

12. 論到電腦技術，沒有多少人能望他項背。

_____

（13）**in one's own right** 憑本身的條件；因自身的能力（14段）

...that the professor had passed much of his knowledge down to me and that I was already a renowned professor in my own right...
……（他知道）我是這位名教授的親傳弟子，也已是大牌教授……

解析

人生常常會有在他人屋簷下，不得不低頭的時刻。怎麼面對呢？把眼光放遠，耐著性子慢慢熬，或許終有出頭之日。等到獨當一面之時，不需要再處處仰人鼻息、看人臉色。英文的 in one's own right 就多少把這個「自成一家」或「獨當一面」的意涵表現出來。

小試身手

13. 他已不只是個學徒（apprentice），乃因自己的能力成了熟練的鐵匠。

_____

（14）do a thorough search on one's computer（15段）

I did a thorough search on my computer, but...
我利用電腦作了大規模的文獻搜尋，……

解析

要利用電腦找什麼資料，只在要搜尋引擎輸入關鍵字，敲一下 enter 鍵，相關資料馬上呈現出來。這個「搜尋」欄，英文就是 search。把搜尋到的資料做一番過濾、整理、分析，英文叫作 do a research job。所以 search 只是搜尋、搜索，並沒有深入去比對資料的意味，但是 research 則不然，反覆地（re-）搜索（search），深入的比對分析資料，「研究」的意思就呈現出來了。另外，一般而言，search 為可數名詞，所以前面常置冠詞 a(n)，但是 research 則為不可數名詞。

還有，請讀者們不要把片語裡的 thorough 和介詞 through「穿（透）過」或連接詞 though「雖然」搞混在一起。thorough 為形容詞，是「徹底的」、「完整的」之意，在這裡和 extensive「廣泛的」、「大規模的」意思接近，用法互通。所以，也可以說成 do an extensive search。

至於 on one's computer 使用介詞 on，這方面也不乏有例可援，「講電話」的英文為 talk on the phone 即是一例。

小試身手

14. 我利用電腦做大規模（extensive）搜尋，設法找到關於該疾病（disease）的資料。

_____

（15）as far as someone can recall 就某人記憶所及；就某人所能回想（15段）

As far as I could recall, the professor had never mentioned this secret experiment to me...

據我記憶所及，這位名教授也從未向我提起這一個秘密的實驗……

解析

這是個很有意思的句型，其實它是個副詞子句。也許我們可以從以下一個比較熟悉和簡單的例子來了解這個句型。

◈ 他說他用完晚餐就會儘快過來。
He said he would come over as soon as he finished dinner.

這麼說來，as far as someone can recall 不就呈現出「儘某人所能深、廣、遠地去回想」這樣的語意來了嗎？而這也就是「就某人記憶所及」，是不是呢？

在此我們用更多例子來熟悉「as far as + 主詞 + 動詞」這個結構：

◈Nothing but desert as far as the eye can see.
◈As far as I know, everything he says is a lie.

15. 據我所能辨別(tell)，我們學校沒有什麼問題。

_____

(16) as a gesture of(respect)為了表示(尊重)；以表達(敬意)(16段)

...as a gesture of respect, the university had asked his widow to donate all his work logs to them.

校方為了表示對他的尊重，曾經請他的遺孀捐出所有他的工作日誌。

解析

gesture 本意為肢體的「姿態」，尤其強調「手勢」，人為什麼要擺姿態、比手勢？當然「表情」是為了要「達意」，所以 gesture 在這個片語中，就很接近中文的「表示」。「表示敬意」英文為 a gesture of respect；而「以之為」表示敬意，「作為」表示敬意，英文為 as a gesture of respect。

16. 我點頭表示同意。

_____

(17) thumb through page by page 逐頁地翻(書或雜誌)；一頁一頁地翻(16段)

...I thumbed through page by page until...

……(我)一頁一頁地看，果然……

解析

舉起你萬能的雙手,看看它們,小指是 little finger,無名指是 ring finger(戒環指)中指是 middle finger,食指是 index finger,而 thumb 為拇指。翻書翻雜誌,你會用到那個指頭呢?當然拇指食指並用,哪一個重要呢?是拇指比較重要吧。你不妨用食指搭配其他指頭翻書看看,很不順手,很不容易吧。所以「翻頁」英文就把 thumb 拿來當動詞用,而以 thumb through the pages 表示之。讀者們在這個要點解析所看到的 thumb through page by page 則表示「逐頁翻」、「一頁一頁地翻」。

小試身手

17. 我把雜誌翻了一翻,直到看膩。

_____

(18) figure the whole thing out 把(整個事情)弄個水落石出;弄清楚來龍去脈(18段)

I told him that I had figured the whole thing out and prescribed a drug to solve his problem.

我告訴他我已弄清楚這是怎麼一回事,因此我已對症下藥。

解析

數學常是學生畏懼的科目,題目一看完,認真算了半天,怎麼都解不出答案來。喔,「計算出來」,這不就是 figure out 嗎?以下這句話常出現在學生的聊天裡,你知道怎麼以英文來表達嗎?

◈ 這道數學題目計算複雜。沒有幾個人算得出來。
This math problem involves complicated calculations. Few people are able to figure it out.

從「計算出來」這個基本意義出發,你就不難理解出另一個含意「搞懂、弄

清楚」。然而，浩瀚宇宙大歸大，其中奧妙還是會讓科學家揭開。人心這個小世界就不同了，真是幽微難明，當事人不講，他人只能妄猜和臆測，難怪有人作一首「其實你不懂我的心」。讀者們，請看完以下的句子再試身手吧。

◈ 我想我永遠搞不懂他行為背後的動機。
I don't think I'll ever be able to figure out the motives behind his behavior.

> **小試身手**
>
> 18. 整個事情很複雜，我弄不懂。
>
> _____

（19）gain a deeper understanding of... 更加／更深入了解……（21段）

But he shared the family's pain throughout their ordeal, and he gained a deeper understanding of death.
可是他卻從頭到尾分擔大家的痛苦，也使他對死亡有深一層的了解。

解析

share 有「分享」、「共有」、「共用」的意思，兄和弟、姊和妹同住一個臥室叫 share a bedroom，和好友共吃一個便當叫作 share a lunchbox 等等。

再講到 gain a deeper understanding of，把動詞 understand 改成名詞 understanding 有它的好處，即方便在它之前加個形容詞 deeper，也可寫成 gain a better understanding of。

小試身手

19. 慢慢地我了解到真愛是怎麼一回事。

_____

(20) be overjoyed to V... 某人（因某事而）大為高興（22段）

...and he was overjoyed to see his test scores go way up as a result.

這位國中生的考試成績，果真大為進步，使他高興極了。

解析

在這裡 overjoyed 是形容詞，意思為「高興得不得了」，強調欣喜的程度超越一般標準，英文另外有個字叫 thrilled 也可以表示類似的情緒。

這個句型另外尚有幾處讀者們要積極學習的地方，一個是「考試成績」test score(s)，一個是「（很有）進步」go way up，另一個為 as a result 相當於「因此」、「因而」。從以上解析來看，整句話的本意是：看到那個孩子（國中生）的成績因（請了家教）而大有進步，令他大為高興。

看到別人成功，是不是會產生酸溜溜、不是滋味的心理呢？其實是正常現象，不要太過就好了。祝福你小試身手成功！

小試身手

20. 除了我以外，其他每個人得知他奪冠（championship）似乎都大為高興。

_____

（21）nothing more than... 只是……；不過是……（25段）

I was forced to admit that the pills I had given him were really nothing more than vitamins.

我只好告訴他，我其實給了他維他命而已。

解析

對於讀者來說，「只是」和「不過是」語意差別不大，幾乎都一樣的意思。這裡我們就利用第二個解釋「不過是……」來弄懂這個片語。請想想看，nothing 是否就是「無物」，而 more than 表示「（超）過」呢？那麼 nothing more than... 即表「不過是……」的意思。由此可見，大部分的英文片語並非都是那麼無厘頭。除了這個，你或許會想到另一個片語 nothing but 吧。沒錯，它也是一樣的意思。以下練習買一送一（buy one and get one free），建議你在第二個題目裡使用 nothing but 來一展身手。

小試身手

21-1. 他安慰我，說那只不過是樹葉在風中抖動（rustle）的聲音。

_____

21-2. 他只關心他自己的利益（interest）。

_____

（22）bear sole responsibility for... 負全責；自行負責（25段）

Man is a creature of free will; each person bears sole responsibility for the good or evil he chooses to do.

人是有自由意志的；行善或行惡，都是人自己的事。

解析

動詞 bear 為「承擔」或「負荷」，再通俗一點說，就是「扛（起來）」。「扛起……的責任來」自然就是 bear responsibility for...。

sole 的本意是「單獨的」、「唯一的」，所以 bear sole responsibility 自然就是「一肩挑起所有責任」。

小試身手

22-1. 在你這年紀你應該為你所言所行負全責。

_____

22-2. 這個責任非我一人所能承擔。

_____

（23）at the cost of... 以……為代價；付出……的代價（25段）

When my patient was young, the only thing he wanted was success, even if it came at the cost of losing the ability to love.

我的病人年輕時，就只想成功，即使不能愛人，也在所不惜。

解析

很希望讀者們學習英文的過程中拋棄一個不好的習慣，就是不要把英文單字「定於一義」。英文單字往往是一字多義的，book 就只當作「書」解釋嗎？pen 就只能解釋成「筆」嗎？name 除了具有「名字」的定義，至少還有幾個其他的意思吧。這個重點裡的 cost 也是如此，它有「花費」、「耗費」的意思，但在這裡不是這個意義。在這裡它作「成本」或「代價」解釋。以下這句英文希望你看得懂：He joked that he got admitted to such a prestigious college at the cost of many nights' sleep.

小試身手

23. 他事業成功卻犧牲掉健康。

_____

（24）never once + 倒裝結構（26段）

We all know Hitler did all kinds of bad things, but never once have we heard he did them because he was controlled by a drug.

我們都知道希特勒做了很多壞事，可是沒有聽說他是在某一種藥物控制之下做的。

解析

原來的句子應該字序如下：...we have never once heard he did them...，但是為了讓讀者或聽者把焦點放在「一次都沒有」，特別就把這個 never once 從放在現在完成式中間的位置（have never once heard）調動到開頭的位置，因為有了這種不尋常的位置異動（否定副詞移至句首），連帶產生的影響是主詞和動詞的部分要倒裝（we have heard → have we heard）。讀者宜多加注意這種「否定副詞（片語）＋倒裝」的句型，它在英文裡很重要，也很常見。

小試身手

24. 我讀高中時物理考試沒一次及格過。

_____

(25) have (time) off（某個時間）不用工作；休假／息(33段)

He must have known the driver would appreciate having the night off.
大概他知道司機晚上要休息的。

解析

在學習這個片語之前，先來了解另一個片語 off duty，它的意思為「下班」、「不值班」，當然反向意義的片語就是 on duty，讀者應不難了解其含意。讀者若從以上的說明掌握到 off 的含意，那麼要學會 have (time) off 就不是難事了。

小試身手

25. 我下午需要請假看牙醫。（過去式）

_____

 小試身手解答

1. Though it's nothing confidential, I'm determined to keep it secret.

2. The doctor is renowned for his great skill in operating on the brain.

3. Her new movie has been the object of much criticism.

4. She was bent on making her first million dollars before thirty.

5. Given his stupidity, he's not going to get rich unless he gets lucky.

6. He rose to prominence at an early age.

7. His shyness rendered him unable to socialize comfortably with others.

8-1. Her parents want her to become a doctor, but she has her heart set on an art career.

8-2. Only a very small percentage of people are able to make a name for themselves in this world.

9. Given how much we've been using the air conditioner, it's hardly surprising (that) our electric bill is so high.

10. She wasn't a fast runner at first, but she improved by leaps and bounds.

11. With a touch of the magic wand, the ogre was transformed back into a beautiful princess.

12. When it comes to computer skills, not many people can measure up to him.

13. No longer a mere apprentice, he's now a master blacksmith in his own right.

14. I did an extensive search on the computer, trying to find information about the disease.

15. As far as I can tell, our school doesn't have any problems.

16. I nodded my head as a gesture of agreement.

17. I thumbed through the magazine until I got tired of looking at it.

18. The whole thing is so complicated (that) I can't figure it out.

19. Gradually I gained an understanding of what true love is all about.

20. Everybody but me seemed to be overjoyed to learn that he won the championship.

21-1. He comforted me by saying it was nothing more than (the sound of) the leaves rustling in the wind.

21-2. He cares about nothing but his own interests.

22-1. At your age you ought to bear sole responsibility for what you do and say.

22-2. The responsibility is more than I can bear alone.

23. He achieved his professional success at the cost of his health.

24. Never once was I able to pass a physics test when I was in high school.

25. I took the afternoon off to visit the dentist.

I'm Only Eight Years Old
我只有八歲

1-5　　我是盧安達的一個小孩，我只有八歲。

　　我們盧安達不是個有錢的國家，可是我運氣很好，過去一直過得很愉快。爸爸是位小學老師，我就在這所小學念書，放了學，我們小孩子都在家附近的田野玩。家附近有樹林，也有一條河。我大概五歲起就會游泳了，在我們這些小孩子中，我不僅游得最好，也跑得最快。

　　因為是鄉下，我們附近有不少的動物，我最喜歡看的是老鷹，牠們飛的姿態真夠優雅。可是我也很怕老鷹，因為牠們常常俯衝下來抓小動物，有一次，有一隻小山貓被一隻大老鷹活活抓走。

　　有一次我問媽媽：「媽媽，大老鷹會不會把小孩抓走？」

　　媽媽說：「傻孩子，小孩子總有大人在旁邊，老鷹不敢抓小孩，因為牠們知道大人一定會保護小孩子的。」

6-10　　我懂了，所以我永遠不敢離開家太遠，我怕老鷹把我抓走。

　　今年，我開始讀報了，看到報上名人的照片，我老是想，有一天我

CD2-7　◇ elementary school 小學；國民小學　　◇ hawk (n.) 鷹

I'm a Rwandan boy, and I'm only eight years old.

Rwanda is not a rich country, but I was lucky—my life was always happy. My dad was a teacher at my elementary school. Every day after school got out, we children liked to play in the fields around our houses. By my house, there was a grove of trees and a river, too. I've known how to swim since I was about five, and not only was I the best swimmer of all the kids, but I was the fastest runner, too.

Because we lived in the country, there were lots of animals around. My favorite ones to watch were the hawks—they flew so gracefully! But I was afraid of hawks, too, because they'd often dive down and pick off smaller animals. Once I saw a little bobcat get carried off alive by a big hawk.

One time I asked my mom, "Mom, do hawks ever carry away little kids?"

Mom replied, "Silly boy! Wherever there are kids, there are always grownups somewhere close by. Hawks don't dare to attack kids because they know the grownups will protect them."

I understood. And so I never dared to stray very far from home for fear that a hawk might carry me away.

This year, I started reading the newspaper. Whenever I saw pictures

◇ grownup(n.)成人；大人
◇ dare(v.)敢；有膽量

◇ protect(v.)保護
◇ stray(v.)亂走／跑

的照片能上報多好。我的親戚朋友們都說我是個漂亮小孩，也許有一天我會像邁可傑克森一樣地有名，報上常常登我的照片。

三星期前，爸爸忽然告訴我們，我們的總統遇難了，他認為事態嚴重。因為有心政客可能乘機將事情越搞越糟。

有一天，爸爸在吃晚飯的時候，告訴我和媽媽，國家隨時可能有內亂，萬一如此，我們要趕快逃離盧安達，到薩伊去。他叫媽媽準備一下逃難時要帶的衣物。

就在那天晚上，一群不知道哪兒來的士兵進入了我們的村子，我睡著了，什麼都不知道，第二天早上才知道，村子裡所有的男人都被打死了，爸爸也不例外。

11-15 媽媽居然還有能力將爸爸埋葬了，當天下午我們開始流亡。現在回想起來，媽媽平時是一位很軟弱的人，這次忽然顯得非常剛強，唯一的理由是因為她要將我送到安全地帶去。媽媽在路上，一再地叮嚀

◇ celebrity（n.）名人
◇ assassinate（v.）暗殺
◇ scheming politician 工於心計的政客
◇ mess（n.）混亂
◇ turmoil（n.）動盪；動亂不安
◇ flee（v.）逃
◇ necessities（n.）必需品；所需之物
◇ beat（v.）毆打（文中 beaten 為 beat 的過去分詞）
◇ include（v.）包括……在內

of celebrities there, I'd always think how cool it would be if my picture were in the newspaper someday. My friends and relatives all said I was a good-looking boy—maybe one day I'd be as famous as Michael Jackson, and my picture would be in the paper all the time.

Then, out of the blue, three weeks ago Dad told us that our president had been assassinated. He thought the country was in serious danger because there were scheming politicians who might use this opportunity to make a real mess of things.

One day while Dad was eating dinner, he told me and Mom that the country might be thrown into turmoil at any moment. If that were to happen, he said, we should hurry and flee Rwanda for Zaire. He told Mom to prepare clothes and necessities to take with us in the event that we did have to flee.

That night, a bunch of soldiers from who knows where came into our village. I was asleep when they came, so it wasn't until the morning that I found out they had beaten every man in the village to death, including my dad.

Somehow my mom found the strength to bury my dad. Then we became refugees—we left our home that afternoon. Thinking about it now, I realize that Mom was a fairly fragile person, but her determination to get me to a safe place made her incredibly strong that

11-15

◇ bury [ˈbɛrɪ] (v.) 埋；葬
◇ refugee [ˌrɛfjʊˈdʒi] (n.) 難民；逃難的人
◇ fragile (adj.) 身體孱弱的
◇ determination (n.) 決心
◇ incredibly (adv.) 難以置信地；難以想像地

我，有人非常恨我們，因此如果發現有壞人來了，可能來不及跑，可是我是小孩子，跑得飛快，一定要拚老命地逃走。媽媽也一再叫我找一棵樹，或者一塊大石頭，以便躲起來，讓壞人看不到。

　　就在逃亡的第二天，壞人來了，媽媽叫我趕快逃，她自己反而不走，我找到了一棵大樹，躲在樹後面，可是我看到了那些壞人殺人的整個過程。媽媽當然也死了，這批士兵沒有留一個人，不像上次，上次他們只殺男人，這次沒有一個人能逃過。

　　士兵走了以後，我才回去看我的媽媽。看到媽媽死了，我大哭了起來，因為天快暗了，我怎麼辦？我只有八歲！

　　虧得還有一個大哥哥也活著，我猜他大概有十幾歲，是個又高又壯的年輕人，剛才他一定也躲了起來，他看我好可憐，來拉我走，他說我們一定要趕快走，找到另一個逃亡的團體，人不能落了單。

　　我和這位大哥哥相依為命，也找到了一批逃亡的人，好幾次有救濟團體給我們東西吃，雖然很少，可是都虧得這位大哥哥，替我弄到食

◇ worth（adj.）價值

day. On the road, Mom warned me again and again that there were people who hated us very much. She said that if we saw bad men coming, we might not have enough time to run away, but since I was a boy and could run like the wind, I should run for all I was worth, find a tree or a big rock, and hide behind it so the bad men wouldn't see me.

On our second day as refugees, the bad men came. Mom told me to run away fast, but she herself didn't run. I found a big tree to hide behind, but I could still see the bad men as they killed the group of people I had been with. Mom died too, of course—these soldiers left no one alive. It wasn't like the last time, when they only killed the men—this time, no one escaped.

After the soldiers left, I went back to see my mom. When I saw her lying there dead, I started crying hard—it was almost dark, and I didn't know what to do. I'm only eight years old!

Luckily, there was another survivor, a tall, strong boy who was older than me (he must have been at least ten). He must have escaped by hiding like I had. He saw how pitiful I looked, so he took me with him. "We have to hurry and find another group of refugees," he said. "We can't let ourselves get left behind!"

My new big brother and I relied on each other to stay alive until we found another group of refugees. We met many aid groups that gave us food to eat, even though it wasn't much, but my main provider was

◇ survivor (n.) 倖存者；生還者　　　　　　◇ provider (n.) 照顧衣食的人；養育之人

物吃，如果不是他的話，我早就餓死了，因為小孩子是很難拿到食物的。

16-20　由於我們大半處於飢餓狀態，我們都越來越瘦，這位大哥哥也不是壯漢了。有一天，他說他要去一條河邊喝水，我告訴他最好忍一下，因為河裡都有過死屍，他說他渴得吃不消，一定要去冒一下險。

當天大哥哥就大吐特吐起來，而且虛弱得走不動了。他要休息，然後勸我不要管他，和其他大人一起繼續逃亡。這次我堅決不肯，決定陪他，他到後來連跟我吵的力氣都沒有了。我偷偷地摸了他的額頭，發現他額頭好燙。

大哥哥昏睡以後，我也睡著了。等我醒過來，我知道他已永遠的離開我了。

我和大哥哥說了再見以後，走回了大路，不知道什麼原因，我從此沒有看到流亡的難民，我只有一片麵包，兩天內，我只吃了這一片麵包，我已越來越走不動了。

◇ starve (v.) 挨餓　　　　　　　　　◇ hold out 苦撐

my big brother, who would find food for me. If it hadn't been for him, I would have starved to death long ago—a little kid can't find much food on his own.

Most of us were still hungry, though. We all got skinnier and skinnier; soon my big brother was no longer the strong, healthy boy he used to be. One day, he said he was going to drink from a river, but I told him it would be better to hold out for a while longer since there had been dead bodies in the water. He said he was so thirsty he couldn't stand it—he had to take the risk.

16-20

Later that day, my big brother started vomiting like crazy and got so weak that he couldn't walk. He had to stop and rest, but he urged me to leave him behind so I could stay with the rest of our group. This time I flatly refused—I had made up my mind to stay with him. Soon he didn't even have the strength to argue with me anymore. I felt his forehead and found that it was burning hot.

After he drifted off, I fell asleep too. When I woke up, I knew he had left me forever.

After saying goodbye to my brother, I walked back to the main road. I don't know why, but I never saw any more groups of refugees after that. All I had was a piece of bread—it was the only food I got to eat for two days. It was getting harder and harder for me to walk.

◇ thirsty (adj.) 口渴的
◇ stand (v.) 忍受；忍耐
◇ risk (n.) 風險；危險

◇ vomit ['vɑmɪt] (v.) 嘔吐
◇ flatly refuse 斷然拒絕
◇ argue (v.) 爭論；爭辯

就在這時候，我發現一頭大老鷹在跟著我，它原來在天上飛，後來發現我越走越慢，索性飛到了地面，我走牠也走，我停牠也停。

21-25　雖然沒有見到任何逃亡潮，卻看到了一部吉普車開過來，我高興極了，以為他們會救我一命，可是吉普車沒有停，我心裡難過到了極點。

吉普車開過去以後，忽然停了下來，車上有人走下來，我的希望又來了。可是那位先生並沒有來救我，他拿起一架配有望遠鏡頭的照相機對著我拍照，當時那隻大老鷹站在我附近。照完以後，吉普車又走了。

我這才想起這位先生一定是一位記者，他要趕回去，使全世界的報紙都會登到這一照片，老鷹在等著小孩過世。明天早上，你們在吃豐盛早飯的時候，就會在報紙上看到我的照片，我不是很希望能上報嗎？這次果真如了願。

你們看到的是一個瘦得皮包骨的小孩，已經不能動了。可是我過去曾是個快樂、漂亮而又強壯的小男孩，我曾經也有父母親隨時陪在我

◇ glide（v.）（鳥在天空）飛行；翱翔　　　◇ approach（v.）接近

It was then I noticed that a big hawk had been following me. At first, he glided along above me, but when he saw how I was slowing down, he went ahead and landed on the ground behind me. When I walked, he'd walk; when I stopped, he'd stop.

21-25

Even though I didn't see a single refugee, I did see a jeep approaching. "They'll save my life!" I thought, overwhelmed with relief. But the jeep drove right on by without stopping. I was heartbroken.

After the jeep had passed me, it suddenly stopped, and a man got out of the car. For a moment, my hope returned. But the man hadn't come to save me—instead, he pulled out a zoom-lens camera and snapped a picture of me as the hawk was standing close by. Once he'd finished, the jeep drove off again.

Then I realized that the man must be a reporter. Right now he's hurrying back to town so that newspapers around the world will publish his picture of a hawk waiting for a child to die. When you eat your big breakfasts tomorrow morning, you'll see my picture in your newspapers. But that's what I've been wishing for, right? Now my wish is about to come true.

What you see will be a bony, emaciated child who can hardly move. But I was once a happy, healthy and handsome boy. Once I had a mother and father who were never far from my side—a hawk would

◇ relief (n.) 放心；安心
◇ heartbroken (adj.) 傷心的；心碎的
◇ zoom-lens camera 變焦鏡頭相機
◇ publish (v.) 刊登
◇ emaciated [ɪˈmeʃɪˌetɪd] (adj.) 瘦弱的

的身旁，使老鷹不敢接近我。我曾經全身充滿了精力，每天在河裡游泳。

現在，我只有一個願望，在老鷹來啄我的時候，我已不會感到痛。

never have dared to come near me then. Once I was full of energy, and I swam in the river every day.

Now I have only one hope left: that when the hawk starts to peck away my flesh, I won't be able to feel any pain.

◇ peck (v.) 啄

（1）after school got out... 放學後……（2段）

Every day after school got out, we children liked to play in the fields around our houses.

（每天）放了學，我們小孩子都在家附近的田野玩。

解析

「放學」可以用 get out of school 這個片語來表達。如果要用子句可以說 when school is over。今天譯者讓我們開了眼界，原來放學也可以這麼表達：after school gets out，英文不拘泥一說的靈活面由此可見。

小試身手

1. 我的學校三點就放學，可是我妹妹的四點才放學。

_____

（2）the best... of all（the kids）在全部的（小孩）當中是最棒的（2段）

I've known how to swim since I was about five, and not only was I the best swimmer of all the kids, but I was the fastest runner, too.

我大概五歲起就會游泳了，在我們這些小孩子中，我不僅游得最好，也跑得最快。

解析

最高級形容詞的後面常常出現 of all，理由其實很自然，當然在「全部」或「所有」當中才會出現「最……」。在這裡舉個例子，這是個臥虎藏龍的資優班，一個段考考下來，人人數學都九十分以上，但是你的朋友拔得頭籌，考了滿分，把眾多高手硬是比下去了，這時你就可以說：My friend got the highest math score of all the students in the class.

2. 藍鯨是所有哺乳類中最大的嗎？

_____

(3) Where(ver)there are..., there are... 有……的地方，就有 ……（5段）

Wherever there are kids, there are always grownups somewhere close by.

小孩子總有大人在旁邊。

解析

看到這句英譯，讀者是否想到千古名句：「有志者事竟成。」呢—— Where there's a will, there's a way. 原來「有志者事竟成。」指的是只要「有決心、有意志」(there is a will) 就會「有條（通向成功的）路」(there is a way)。那麼格言開頭的 where 又是怎麼回事呢？它是連接詞，負責把兩個子句串連起來。其實，用其他的連接詞如 when 和 if 取代 where 也可，只是既然是千古名言，所以還是維持用 where 吧。

想要在寫作裡用上一句「有工廠就有污染」嗎？怎麼辦，如底下的句子就是了。

◇Where there are factories, there is pollution.

3. 有山的地方總會有爬山的人。

_____

（4） for fear that... 唯恐⋯⋯（6段）

And so I never dared to stray very far from home for fear that a hawk might carry me away.

所以我永遠不敢離開家太遠，我怕老鷹把我抓走。

解析

建議讀者把 for fear that 整個當成連接詞來看（註：當然 that 本身已經是連接詞了），這個連接詞表示「唯恐」的意思也很自然，因為 fear 即是「恐懼」、「害怕」之意。相反的，如果你做了某事，滿心希望有什麼結果，可以考慮使用 in the hope that... 比如：

◈ I wrote him a letter in the hope that he would reply and tell me what to do next.

小試身手

4. 他用掛號寄那封信，不然他怕信會寄丟了。

_____

（5） make a real mess of things 製造混亂；大鬧一場（8段）

...there were scheming politicians who might use this opportunity to make a real mess of things.

⋯⋯有心政客可能乘機將事情越搞越糟。

解析

mess 作名詞解為「亂的狀態」。父母有時心血來潮，看一下孩子房間，通常會 cannot believe their eyes 然後無助地內心吶喊 Oh, dear God! What a mess! 因此，這個解析重點的 make a real mess of things 自然就是「製造混亂」或「搞得亂七八糟」的意思。

另外要注意，mess 亦可作動詞解，意思是「弄糟」、「搞亂」，常和介副詞 up 合用。比如 Don't mess up the things on my desk. 意思為「別亂動我桌上的東西。」

小試身手

5. 學生們因為把實驗室搞得亂七八糟而被申誡（reprimanded）。

_____

(6) be thrown into turmoil 陷入混亂（9段）

One day while Dad was eating dinner, he told me and Mom that the country might be thrown into turmoil at any moment.

有一天，爸爸在吃晚飯的時候，告訴我和媽媽，國家隨時可能有內亂。

解析

名詞 turmoil 的原意為「動盪不安」、「混亂無序」，因此片語 be thrown into turmoil 就是「陷入混亂」、「動盪不已」。請再多看一個例句：

◆ 國家隨時可能有內亂。
Civil war might break out at any moment.

小試身手

6. 她身陷感情困擾，花了好久時間才恢復過來。

_____

(7) in the event that... 如果……；萬一……（9段）

He told Mom to prepare clothes and necessities to take with us in the event that we did have to flee.

他叫媽媽準備一下逃難時要帶的衣物。

解析

看到這個解析重點，會不會令你覺得和之前的重點四很相近呢？沒錯，重點四的 for fear that... 整個可以當成連接詞看，這裡的 in the event that... 也可整個視為連接詞，它非常像連接詞 if，但是更常用來指某種某人所不樂於見到，或是不希望發生的情況。

比如氣象預報說明天是好天氣，適合各種娛樂或體育活動，你是比賽承辦人，為了考慮周延，可以告知參賽隊伍：「如果下雨，就把比賽移到室內進行。」以英文表示為：We'll move the games indoors in the event that it rains.

小試身手

7. 警察奉命，倘若示威者使用暴力，要予以反擊。

_____

---

(8) who knows where 沒人知道的地方；鬼才知道的地方（10段）

That night, a bunch of soldiers from who knows where came into our village.

就在那天晚上，一群不知道哪兒來的士兵進入了我們的村子。

解析

「誰知道？」(Who knows?) 其實常用來表示「沒人知道」(Nobody knows.) 或「我不知道」(I don't know.) 的意思。因此，這裡的 who knows where 其實相當於 (I don't know where) 或 (nobody knows where)。

小試身手

8. 未來會帶來些什麼，誰也不知道。

_____

（9）run like the wind 快跑如風（11段）

run for all one's worth 死命地跑；沒命地跑

...but since I was a boy and could run like the wind, I should run for all I was worth, find a tree or a big rock, and hide behind it so the bad men wouldn't see me.

可是我是小孩子，跑得飛快，一定要拚老命地逃走。（媽媽也一再叫我）找一棵樹，或者一塊大石頭，以便躲起來，讓壞人看不到。

解析

這是個很有趣的英文用語，很生動地把高速快跑的畫面以文字呈現給讀者和聽者。中文用「來如電，去如風」來描寫來去動作之迅速，豐富的英文當然也有這樣的語彙，用心領悟，想想 run like the wind ，你應該有個會心的微笑。動物世界裡，哪種動物飛奔的速度最快呢？是印度豹吧，所以當然也可以說 I can run like a cheetah. 另外的一個片語 run for all one is worth 意思則稍有不同。這個片語強調逃命似地跑，再不快跑，則禍難臨頭，甚至有生命之憂，也就是這個片語帶有 run for your life 和 run as fast as you can 的味道，和只著重在奔跑的速度是有區別的。

小試身手

9. 當可怕的海嘯（tsunami）滾滾而來，所有在海灘度假的遊客奔逃保命。

_____

（10）leave no one alive 沒有留下一個活口；趕盡殺絕（12段）

Mom died too, of course—these soldiers left no one alive.

媽媽當然也死了，這批士兵沒有留一個人。

解析

leave no one alive 作「沒有留下一個活口」或「趕盡殺絕」解並不難學，但這裡我們要留意的是動詞的用法。請看以下兩個例子：

◈ 他走出屋子，門沒關上。
He went out of the house, leaving the door open.

◈ 他不留情的批評讓我感到沮喪。
His relentless criticism left me feeling discouraged.

由此可見，動詞 leave 在此類的用法裡相當於「讓某事或某人處於某狀態」的意思。

小試身手

10. 別讓這些植物受烈日照射太久。

_____

（11）If it hadn't been for... 若非……；要不是因為……（15段）

If it hadn't been for him, I would have starved to death long ago...

如果不是他的話，我早就餓死了……

解析

除了本解析重點的 If it hadn't been for... 表示「若非……」或「要不是因為……」，另一個常見的句型是 If it weren't for...。兩者皆表示「與事實相反」的情況，但是兩者的用法卻是大大不同，而最大的不同處則在「時間」的意

涵。If it hadn't been for... 用在時間為「過去」時，而 If it weren't for... 用在時間為「現在」。與事實相反的假設在前兩輯有很詳細的討論，所以此處僅作扼要的說明，讀者用心，仍然可以體會其中的微妙。

上週三上班時因為出了點小意外，沒有趕上火車。現在和好友談到此事，不免牢騷一句：「要不是因為那個小意外，我就不會錯過火車了。」因為這是過去（上週三）的事情，所以得選擇 If it hadn't been for... 表達整句，即：If it hadn't been for that little accident, I would've caught the train.

有人要向你借錢，你本生性慷慨，但對方實在態度欠佳，讓你反感，這時不妨正色告訴對方：「要不是因為你的態度，我可能會借些現金給你。」因為這是當前的事情，所以得使用 If it were not for... 來表達，句子寫成：If it weren't for your（bad）attitude, I might lend you some cash.

以下的練習，你會選擇哪一個句型呢？

小試身手

11. 如果沒有網際網路，我們就無法用電子郵件溝通。

_____

（12）take the risk 冒險（16段）

He said he was so thirsty he couldn't stand it—he had to take the risk.
他說他渴得吃不消，一定要去冒一下險。

解析

三個重點：

(1)so...(that)... ：如此……以致……。
(2)can't stand it ：無法忍耐。動詞 stand 在此為「忍耐」的意思。
(3)take the risk ，是「冒這個險」的意思。

小試身手

12-1. 她美到沒有人能不轉頭看她。

_____

12-2. 你怎麼受得了這麼潮濕的天氣？

_____

12-3. 我知道我們機會不大，但若不冒點險，我們就不會有進展。

_____

（13）**V like crazy** 沒命地⋯⋯；不要命地⋯⋯（**17**段）

Later that day, my big brother started vomiting like crazy and got so weak that he couldn't walk.

當天大哥哥就大吐特吐起來，而且虛弱得走不動了。

解析

「大吐特吐」總歸是個「吐」字，如果你是個翻譯工作者，要找個達意的字不難，要兼顧到傳神就不容易了，可見本書的譯者確實有三兩三，在動詞 vomit 之後加個 like crazy 那個「大⋯⋯特⋯⋯」的神韻就顯現出來了。還有一個 like there's no tomorrow（當然這兩種說法都比較口語）也常用來表示這種「大⋯⋯特⋯⋯」的意思，比如：

◆ 考完試後，我和朋友們大玩特玩。

After we finished our exams, my friends and I partied like there was no tomorrow.

除了「大吐特吐」，中文還有「大吃特吃」、「大買特買」，想試試看嗎？

13. 我們進到商場，大買特買。

_____

(14) drift off（悠悠地）**睡著**（18段）

After he drifted off, I fell asleep too.

大哥哥昏睡以後，我也睡著了。

解析

fall asleep 為「入睡」之意，是國高中學生百分之百都學過的重要片語，但 drift off 則不同，它指人在很累很疲憊的情況下，無法控制地「飄飄然／昏昏然入睡」。drift 本意為在水上隨水流而「漂」或在空氣中隨氣流而「飄」。至於怎麼「漂／飄」，往哪裡「漂／飄」、「漂／飄」多快，都是無法自主控制的。有的病人常常一下子清醒，一下子昏迷，這種情形英文以 drift in and out of consciousness 表達，非常的貼切。

小試身手

14. 我沉沉進入美麗的夢鄉，醒來精神飽滿。

_____

(15)（be）overwhelmed with...（21段）

"They'll save my life!" I thought, overwhelmed with relief.

我高興極了，以為他們會救我一命。

解析

（某人）「高興極了」，怎麼表示呢？譯者在此做了很好的示範，用 be

overwhelmed with relief 來詮釋。讀者也許會想，為何不選擇其他表示「高興」的字眼，如 delight, amusement, pleasure, joy, excitement, happiness 等？對於一個身處兵荒馬亂，舉目無親的稚齡兒童來說，看到有人乘吉普車而來，那種心情應該是焦慮後如釋重負的解脫吧，所以選擇用 relief 表達「高興」是很高明的翻譯技巧。另外請讀者特別注意 overwhelmed 這個字，它常和一些表達心情感受的字連用，如 disappointment「失望」、dismay「駭異」、embarrassment「難堪」、gratitude「感激」、guilt「罪惡感」、panic「驚恐」，用以表示某人「滿懷……」、「滿心……」或「……難抑」、「……不已」。

小試身手

15. 他凝視著她，悲傷難抑，難以置信。

_____

---

(16) snap a picture of... 拍張……照片 (22段)

But the man hadn't come to save me—instead, he pulled out a zoom-lens camera and snapped a picture of me as the hawk was standing close by.

可是那位先生並沒有來救我，他拿起一架配有望遠鏡頭的照相機對著我拍照，當時那隻大老鷹站在我附近。

解析

國高中時期學到的「拍……照片」是 take a picture of...，動詞用 take 非常之「正式」，非常之「基本」，但是也非常之「不生動」、「不生活化」。譯者在這句譯文裡使用 snap，整個拍照的動作立即活靈活現的展現在眼前。

女士買完東西付錢後，「啪」地一聲把錢包關上，英文可以表示為 snap her purse shut；若是男士出差，整理行囊，衣服裝好之後，把手提箱順手「啪」一聲關上，英文為 snap the suitcase shut。所以，「啪、啪、啪」按快門拍

照的英文即為 snap a picture of...。

小試身手

16. 遊客們都驚異金字塔之宏偉，開始一張又一張地拍起照來。

＿＿＿＿＿＿＿＿＿＿＿＿＿＿＿＿＿＿＿＿＿＿＿

（17）have only... left 只剩下……（25段）

Now I have only one hope left: that when the hawk starts to peck away my flesh, I won't be able to feel any pain.

現在，我只有一個願望，在老鷹來啄我的時候，我已不會感到痛。

解析

要表達「只剩下……」時，使用來表達最貼切 have only... left 了。一大早進台北城，身上帶著一千塊錢，邊逛邊吃邊買，下午回家時，身上「只剩下」十五塊錢，剛好足以買公車票……。別管怎麼辦，先想想這句話該如何說：

◈ I have only fifteen dollars left, just enough to buy a bus ticket.

人活到老年，最感慨的常是故知舊識一一凋零，好友所剩無幾，小試身手裡的第一個題目就在描述這種淒涼心境，也許你正年輕，但不妨為作練習強說愁，試試看吧。

小試身手

17-1. 他常感傷(lament)在世上好友所剩無幾。

＿＿＿＿＿＿＿＿＿＿＿＿＿＿＿＿＿＿＿＿＿＿＿

17-2. 他從倒塌的屋子逃出，發現(全身)只剩下身上的衣服。

＿＿＿＿＿＿＿＿＿＿＿＿＿＿＿＿＿＿＿＿＿＿＿

小試身手解答

1. I get out of school at 3, but my sister doesn't get out until 4.

2. Is the blue whale the largest of all mammals?

3. Wherever there are mountains, there will be people to climb them.

4. He sent the letter by registered mail for fear that it might get lost otherwise.

5. The students were reprimanded for making a mess of the science laboratory.

6. It took her a long time to recover from the emotional turmoil she was thrown into.

7. The police are instructed to fight back in the event that the demonstrators use violence.

8. Who knows what the future will bring?

9. As the terrible tsunami rolled in, the tourists on the beach ran for their lives.

10. Don't leave the plants exposed to the hot sun for too long.

11. If it weren't for the Internet, we wouldn't be able to communicate with each other by email.

12-1. She is so beautiful that no one can stop looking at her.

12-2. How can you stand such humid weather?

12-3. I know we don't have much chance, but we won't get anywhere if we don't take a little risk.

13.   We went into the mall and shopped like crazy.

14.   I drifted off into a wonderful dream and woke up feeling refreshed.

15.   He stared at her, overwhelmed with grief and disbelief.

16.   All the visitors were amazed at the grandeur of the pyramid and began snapping photo after photo of it.

17-1. He often laments the fact that he has only a few friends left in this world.

17-2. He escaped from the collapsed house, finding all he had left was the clothes on his body.

Linking English
讀李家同學英文3：我只有八歲

2007年4月初版　　　　　　　　　　　　　　　定價：新臺幣250元
2016年6月初版第四刷
有著作權‧翻印必究
Printed in Taiwan.

著　　者	李家同	
譯　　者	Nick Hawkins	
解　　析	周正一	
總 編 輯	胡金倫	
總 經 理	羅國俊	
發 行 人	林載爵	

出　版　者　聯經出版事業股份有限公司　　叢書主編　何采嬪
地　　　址　台北市基隆路一段180號4樓　　校　　對　Nick Hawkins
台北聯經書房　台北市新生南路三段94號　　　　　　　林慧如
電　　　話　（02）23620308　　封面設計　翁國鈞
台中分公司　台中市北區崇德路一段198號
暨門市電話　（04）22312023
郵政劃撥帳戶第0100559-3號
郵 撥 電 話　（02）23620308
印　刷　者　文聯彩色製版印刷有限公司
總　經　銷　聯合發行股份有限公司
發　行　所　新北市新店區寶橋路235巷6弄6號2F
電　　　話　（02）29178022

行政院新聞局出版事業登記證局版臺業字第0130號

本書如有缺頁，破損，倒裝請寄回台北聯經書房更換。　ISBN　978-957-08-3144-3 (平裝)
聯經網址 http://www.linkingbooks.com.tw
電子信箱 e-mail:linking@udngroup.com

國家圖書館出版品預行編目資料

讀李家同學英文 3：我只有八歲
/李家同著 . Nick Hawkins 譯 . 周正一解析 .
初版 . 臺北市：聯經，2007 年（民 96）
232 面；14.8×21 公分 .（Linking English）
ISBN　978-957-08-3144-3（平裝附光碟片）
[2016年6月初版第四刷]

1.英國語言-讀本

805.18　　　　　　　　　　96006108